Murder Fit for a King

Murder Fit for a King

A Dani and Caitlin Mystery

Larry McCloskey

A SANDCASTLE BOOK

A MEMBER OF THE DUNDURN GROUP
TORONTO

Editor: Michael Carroll
Designer: Erin Mallory
Map: Julia Bell
Printer: Webcom

Library and Archives Canada Cataloguing in Publication

McCloskey, Larry
    Murder fit for a king : a Dani and Caitlin mystery / Larry McCloskey.

ISBN 978-1-55002-669-6

    1. King, William Lyon Mackenzie, 1874-1950--Juvenile fiction. I. Title.

PS8575.C635M874 2007   jC813'.6   C2006-904612-3

1   2   3   4   5   11   10   09   08   07

Conseil des Arts du Canada   Canada Council for the Arts

Canada

ONTARIO ARTS COUNCIL
CONSEIL DES ARTS DE L'ONTARIO

We acknowledge the support of the **Canada Council for the Arts** and the **Ontario Arts Council** for our publishing program. We also acknowledge the financial support of the **Government of Canada** through the **Book Publishing Industry Development Program** and **The Association for the Export of Canadian Books**, and the **Government of Ontario** through the **Ontario Book Publishers Tax Credit program** and the **Ontario Media Development Corporation**.

Care has been taken to trace the ownership of copyright material used in this book. The author and the publisher welcome any information enabling them to rectify any references or credits in subsequent editions.

J. Kirk Howard, President

Printed and bound in Canada
www.dundurn.com

Dundurn Press
3 Church Street, Suite 500
Toronto, Ontario, Canada
M5E 1M2

Gazelle Book Services Limited
White Cross Mills
High Town, Lancaster, England
LA1 4XS

Dundurn Press
2250 Military Road
Tonawanda, NY
U.S.A. 14150

For Mar Mar.

And to the Irish families who once lived and farmed in the meadow at the top of McCloskey Road in Gatineau Park until about 1875. High along that rocky, inhospitable ridge of deep forest, as recounted by C.E. Mortureaux in "History of George's Trail" published in the 1923–24 Canadian Ski Annual, "once lived and toiled a little colony of Irish settlers — the Dunlops, Laheys, Keogans, Egans, Jeffs, McGuires, and McCloskeys. How they came to settle on this stony land, no one knows. Probably they were planted here on some dark night and stayed because they did not know that the rest of the world had anything better to offer. One day, as the story goes, they heard from some visitor about the level, flat land in the valley below, and straightaway they packed their household goods and climbed down, never to return, some by McCloskey's Hill and some by Murphy's."

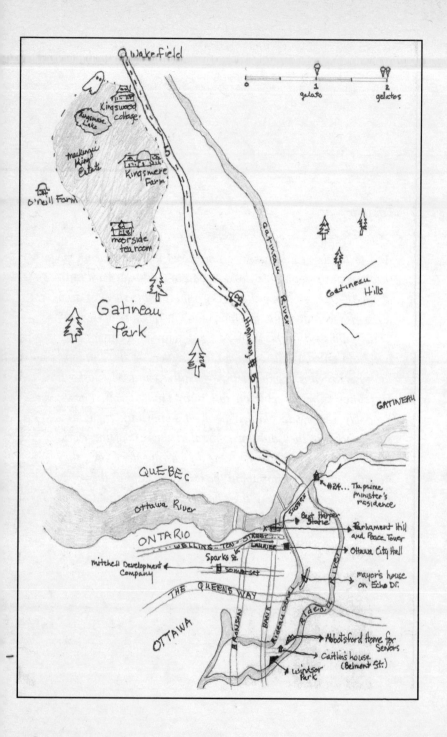

1
A Ghostly Tour

"I'm mad," Dani said, wrinkling her forehead like a distressed beagle.

Dani's beagle, Nikki, howled at a passing squirrel before placing *his* wrinkled forehead between his paws on his master's foot.

Caitlin watched the pair and thought, *They say that if a couple stays together long enough, they begin to look alike. Poor Dani.*

"I'm mad!" Dani repeated, this time with a little more volume and a lot more wrinkles.

"Dani, you can't stay mad at your dad forever. Besides, maybe you'll get to like a cottage closer to Ottawa. Three hours was an awful long time driving to your old cottage."

Dani folded her arms as if hugging herself. "I don't care if another dumb cottage is closer. I want *my* cottage back."

"But, Dani, it's kind of true what your dad said about us asking 'Are we there yet?' every few minutes. Besides, there might be a whole bunch of fun cottages up in the Gatineau Hills like your dad says."

"I don't care, and I'm still mad. I'm not going to look at dumb old cottages. I still can't believe Dad sold *our* cottage. We've had it ever since I was a baby. We went there every year for my birthday and for summer holidays and for Thanksgiving." Dani unfolded her arms and dropped them to her sides, sighing grandly.

"The cottages in the pictures looked pretty cool," Caitlin said.

"I don't care!"

Caitlin could see the gelato Dani's dad, John, had promised for cottage-hunting company melting away. *This will have to be handled very carefully,* she thought. "Dani, if we go look at cottages, we can build a great big pile of leaves and jump in it."

"I don't care about dumb leaves!"

"Dani, we could let Nikki run loose. You know how much he loves that."

"Nikki doesn't care, either."

Caitlin spit out one of her blond braids and thought, *Time to get serious.* "We could go and you could stay mad at your dad and he'll see how rotten every cottage is and maybe he'll buy back your old cottage."

Dani pulled on Nikki's leash and started striding away from her friend.

"Hey, Dani, where are you going?"

"Come on, Caitlin, let's go look at those rotten cottages."

"Ghost tour?" Dani asked through smacking gum.

"That's right." John glanced at the girls in the rearview mirror. "Our tenth prime minister, William Lyon Mackenzie

King, used to spend his summers here in the glorious Gatineau Hills at his estate on Kingsmere Lake. Get it — King at Kingsmere? Anyway, turns out our holder of highest office was a bit of a kook. It seems he spent a fair bit of time chatting with his dead mom." John checked the rearview mirror to see if the girls were suitably impressed.

"Dad, the road, you know," Dani said between gum smackings.

"And don't forget, Mackenzie King was our prime minister during our time of greatest crisis," John continued. "Canada was at war with Germany and Japan, a war we very nearly lost, and during it all, Mackenzie King was probably conversing with his maternal ghost for advice about war and how to run the country. Now that's a spooky piece of history!"

"Dad, are you serious about a ghost tour?" Dani asked. "I thought we were looking at dumb cottages."

"We can look at cottages after the tour, which starts in exactly three minutes. And what better time for a ghost tour than two weeks before Halloween." John pulled the van into a parking lot. "Look, there's a group gathering over there. I'll run over and see if they're here for the ghost tour."

The girls watched as John ran to the group, then dashed back.

Louise, Dani's stepmother, chewed on her sunglasses and mumbled, "I think we'd better get Nikki to teach John how to relax."

"Girls, Louise, come on, the ghost tour's starting. Oh, Dani, better bring Nikki's leash. He might bolt if he gets *spooked*."

John giggled at his own joke as he frantically searched the van for his sunglasses, his hat, and other paraphernalia. Louise, the girls, and Nikki reluctantly joined the back of the group.

"This is going to be boring," Dani said, folding her arms.

"This is going to be interesting," John said, catching up and rubbing his hands together. "Come on, Louise, let's move up closer to the front."

"Oh, joy," Louise muttered, her words lost in the October wind.

"Ladies and gentlemen, welcome to the National Capital Commission's Ghost Tour," an enthusiastic voice boomed, hidden to the girls somewhere on the front lines. "We're pleased to present to you today a fascinating glimpse into Canadian history here at the beautiful Mackenzie King Estate, or as most people call it, Kingsmere."

The tour group spread around the voice until the girls caught sight of a middle-aged man in matching tan shirt, vest, hat, and neatly creased pants. "For it is here that our esteemed prime minister thought about the weighty affairs of Canada and consorted with and was advised by his long-dead mother. In short, ladies and gentlemen, the leader of our country, and Canada's longest-serving prime minister, may have taken counsel from a ghost, or perhaps a series of ghosts, and as such was just plain nuts!" Members of the tour group snickered as the tan man prattled on. "But seriously, folks …"

"Dumb ghost tour," Dani said to Caitlin, tuning out.

"Ha-ha, very smart," John said to no one in particular at the front of the group.

"And finally, to complete today's tour, we'll end up at the Moorside Tearoom just in time for tea and Mrs. Simpson's delectable pumpkin pie." The tan man paused and rubbed his stomach. "Mmm!"

The tour group members responded with an enthusiastic chorus of "Mmm!"

"But first," the tour guide added, "let's stroll down to Kingsmere Lake and see the guest house, or should I say, *ghost* house. Ha, ha, ha …"

Over the noise of the entire group, John could be heard guffawing.

Dani groaned. "Now I'm really mad. Fake ghost tour, fake cottages, fake trees."

"Fake trees?" Caitlin said. Then she thought, *Dani's arms are wrapped so tightly around her that she looks like a mad scientist in a straitjacket.* Caitlin couldn't resist tormenting her friend, so she rubbed her stomach and said, "Mmm!"

Dani moaned and squeezed all the harder.

The voice of the ghost tour guide faded away as the girls drifted farther back. Only one straggler remained on the trail behind the girls.

"Guess we haven't got a ghost of a chance of meeting a real ghost on this fake tour," Caitlin said.

Dani tried to wipe her nose but struggled to untangle her hand from her overall strap. "It's 'cause adults don't believe in ghosts, so they feel they have to make dumb adult jokes about them."

"Yes, yes, you're quite right," a peevish voice behind the girls agreed. "Mind you, I never had children myself to compare with adults. Never did get married. And though I didn't dislike children, I always had a strong preference for a canine companion, as you can see."

The girls rotated slowly toward the tour group straggler. The short, stocky man stood with one hand on his walking stick and the other holding a leash attached to his dog, a small terrier. The straggler was dressed in a tweed suit with long, baggy shorts, high wool socks, and leather hiking shoes. The way the man and his dog held their heads and looked around the estate seemed to indicate they were familiar with the place. As he spoke to the girls, he remained expressionless in spite of his bizarre words.

"Oh, it's true in part what these people say about my peculiarities. But they don't really understand, and under the present circumstances, well, I think I've been proven correct, not that the public cares to take note. So it wasn't a grand delusion, was it?" The odd man ceased his rambling for a moment and stooped to pat his dog on the head. "There, there, Pat." The dog glanced at the object of his affection and wagged his tail.

"Mister, we have to get back to the ghost tour 'cause my dad and my six uncles are waiting for us," Dani said nervously.

At the same time Caitlin thought, *Wow, I wonder if Dani noticed that this is the first dog Nikki hasn't howled at in his entire life!* Then Caitlin cocked her head and asked the strange man, "What exactly wasn't a grand delusion?"

Before the stranger could start speaking again, Dani motioned with her eyes, the signal for getting the heck out of there. Caitlin ignored her friend and listened to the babbling stranger.

"Why, my belief in the afterlife, of course. After all, as you and only you can see, here I am. I'm all but forgotten by young people today, except for an occasional unkind and inaccurate remark they seem to latch on to about my dear mother. But most people can't possibly understand how close my mother and I were, how much I missed her when she died, and what comfort it was to communicate with her on the other side."

Dani was speechless, but her eyes raced through an assortment of expressions, all of which seemed intent on impressing Caitlin with the need to run as if they were being pursued by a pack of wild dogs.

"If she was your mother, and you were close to her, wouldn't she already be on your side?" Caitlin asked, ignoring Dani.

"Indeed," the stranger said thoughtfully, "we are, naturally, on the same side now, but when I served as prime minister, in times of need, we were able to communicate between the worlds of the living and the dead …"

Dani's eyes were now as wide and round as two saucers as she pushed Caitlin down the path toward the ghost tour. "Well, mister, it's been real nice and real instructional meeting you."

The stranger followed the girls, carefully placing his walking stick and peering down at his dog, who happily followed by his master's side. "Still, the notion that I governed the country, particularly through the turbulent war years, on the advice of my mother is preposterous. After all, one's private life and public duties aren't at all the same thing. Those séances were meant to keep my spirits up — pardon the seeming pun — so I could function as a proper prime minister and make decisions for the good of the country. Never in twenty-two years did I allow myself to be influenced by personal matters, let alone …"

The girls watched the stranger stumble through the forest and go past them without looking up until he was quite alone. Suddenly, he became aware of his solitude and cast his eyes around for his audience. Blinking into the sunlight, he appeared lost and confused, then pivoted and skewered his audience of two with new determination. "Perhaps I haven't been as clear as I should. You see, I'm a ghost."

"How, how, how …?" Dani sputtered.

"Who, who, who …?" Caitlin stammered.

The two girls could have been a pair of monkeys speaking like a couple of owls.

"How is a rather complicated question that I can't fully answer, but who is easy. I am William Lyon Mackenzie King, naturally, and this is Pat, my lifetime, uh, ghost-time friend."

"Naturally," Caitlin said, chewing nervously on one of her French braids.

"But, why, why, why …?" Dani continued to splutter.

The stranger's voice became steadier and more self-assured as he spoke. "My purpose is none other than to protect this glorious park. And though less important, I hope to redeem something of my rather muddled reputation. But I can't achieve either of these important goals without your help." The stranger paused for a moment as if lost in thought, then asked a bit ruefully, "By the way, did I mention that doing all this involves solving a rather troublesome murder?"

2
A Sweep and Swirl of Leaves

As Dani and Caitlin tried to catch up to the rest of the tour group now assembled at Kingswood Cottage, they both noticed that Nikki kept looking weirdly at the space occupied by Pat the terrier.

"Dani," Caitlin whispered, "I don't think Nikki can see Pat, but he senses something's there. A ghost dog's so cool, don't you think?"

"Yeah, real cool. That's all we need is another ghost. You're right about Nikki, though. He can't figure it out."

The moment the girls rejoined the tour group the guide continued his carefully worded presentation, which provoked a snort from the little stranger claiming to be Mackenzie King's ghost.

"I've heard this endless prattle many times, and it never ceases to irk me. It's sensationalist fluff, a profound discredit to my dear mother, and an absurd attack on my character and accomplishments as prime minister. The fool says I was crazy at the very place I had the best times of my life. The truth is, there are very few living humans who believe in ghosts. Why, if you think about it, by implication this idiot fellow is also saying that you two young ladies are crazy. After all, I'm a ghost and you can obviously see me."

"We're not crazy!" Dani insisted a bit too loudly.

Heads turned toward the girls, and the tour guide paused in his speech as he searched for the source of the interruption.

"No, of course you're not," John said, glaring at his daughter as if she *were* crazy.

Caitlin shrugged at the staring crowd, trying to give the impression that she was the tolerant, caring friend of a raving lunatic on a day pass from an asylum.

"Don't let them get to you girls," King said. "I always had to endure the taunts and whispers of narrow-minded people because of my particular, uh, eccentricities."

"What are ecc … eccentricities?" Caitlin asked, wrinkling her nose.

"Certain quirky characteristics," John answered as he hurried toward the girls. "I hadn't really thought of you as eccentric, but you *are* kind of quirky, Dani."

"What do you mean?" Dani demanded.

"Well, for example, didn't you wear those long-legged overalls all summer?" Suddenly, John began bouncing from one foot to the other.

"Dad, you're wearing shorts and it's almost snowing." Then she noticed her father hopping around. "The washroom's over there, Dad."

"Right. Back in a flash."

"A grown man needs to be told when and where to go to the washroom and *he* thinks his daughter's a bit weird,"

Louise said, joining the girls.

"Pot calling the kettle black," King offered.

"Huh?" both girls cried loudly.

"It's an expression," King told them.

"I'm sorry. Do you have a question?" the tour guide asked as heads once again craned toward the girls. "Maybe our two young friends would like to lead this tour. Perhaps they'll find a real ghost for us, since they seem to have a lot to contribute today."

Laughter broke out among the tour group members.

The tour guide smirked. "Maybe you know a way to call a ghost on demand just like old Mackenzie King did when he wanted to talk to his mom."

"Blasted fool! Go on, girls, move up to the front of the group and we'll show this nincompoop and his band of doubting Thomases something to remember. Don't worry. I'll back you up whatever you do."

"Cat got your tongue?" the tour guide taunted. "Come now, girls, you seem to want the floor. Now you have it. Tell us or show us something more interesting than I can. Come on, let's see something fantastic."

Slowly, ever so slowly, Caitlin's wrinkles disappeared from her forehead, and the braid she had been chewing dropped from her mouth.

Even more slowly, Dani's scowl vanished and a benevolent smile splashed across her face.

"Show them!" King encouraged.

Twenty pairs of eyes and twenty know-it-all adult smiles were fixed on the girls, waiting and watching.

"Well …" Dani began, folding her arms.

"Well …" Caitlin started, hoping Dani would hurry up and say something.

"Yes, it's true we're here to demonstrate that ghosts really do exist at Mr. King's estate," Dani finally said.

Chuckles greeted her declaration. Returning from the washroom, John looked mortified, just as he did when Nikki peed on the leg of someone Dani's father had stopped to talk to.

Caitlin glanced nervously at her friend as the tour guide's smirk widened. "That's right … I think." Then, shooting a panicked look at Dani, she said, "Now what?"

"I'm not sure," Dani whispered through clenched teeth.

"Offer to move something and I'll do it," King suggested.

"Well, perhaps it's time to return to Earth and get on with the tour," the guide said.

"I can prove a ghost is here," Dani said, "'cause the ghost is going to move that broom over there."

An outburst of giggles was quickly extinguished by deep gasps for air. A broom innocently leaning against the cottage moved ever so slightly as Dani finished speaking. Silence descended on the group before adult common sense quickly reasoned away the fantastic event.

"No, it couldn't have been," someone said.

"It's not possible," another insisted.

"Can't imagine," still another maintained.

Dani hugged herself and put on her maddest expression. "Oh, yeah? Just watch."

Jaws dropped as the broom twirled several times and fell to the ground. Again silence engulfed the group, and Dani's maddest expression was replaced with a grin.

"Now *everyone* looks like a ghost," Caitlin marvelled.

"Way cool," Dani said. "Eat your heart out, Harry Potter."

"The wind!" a woman shouted from the tour group.

"Yeah, that's it," another man said. "The wind blew the broom."

Murmurs and nervous giggles percolated throughout the group.

"Ladies and gentlemen, this little episode has been amusing," the guide said, "but we do have a tour to complete, after all." All business now, the guide briskly shepherded his charges in the direction of Moorside Cottage.

"Almost seemed real …" one man mumbled.

"Had us going, the little dickins," an old geezer said, shaking his head.

"Funny little coincidence …" a woman murmured.

Dani's maddest expression reshaped her face as the tour group entered Moorside Cottage.

I wonder if we'll ever get to the gelato, Caitlin thought.

King huffed and puffed. "Coincidence, my …! If only these grown-up fools realized there's no such thing as coincidence. That guide reminds me of one of my most troublesome ministers. He was all reason and blindness, too."

"Huh?" Caitlin and Dani exclaimed simultaneously.

"Don't you see, young ladies? Most people, all adults I daresay, think the world is what they see before them. They can't imagine anything else, and politicians are the worst."

"How come people vote for them then?" Dani asked.

"Precisely because they, the voting public, want desperately to believe in this rational, predictable, and utterly foolish world."

Caitlin leaned forward and whispered to King in a conspiratorial manner. "Sir, who are the *they* everyone's always talking about?"

"You know, I'm not entirely sure."

Dani rolled her eyes. "None of that matters. What does matter is here comes my dad and he looks frantic, like he wants us to finish giving the ghost tour or something. So,

Mr. King, I think we both would like to know exactly how you think we can help?"

King seemed pensive as Dani spoke and then began to wring his hands. "If only I knew. As prime minister, if I asked a minister for help, it was with the understanding that he had a large and capable staff behind him. I'll tell you what I know when next I get the chance, but for now read your neighbourhood newspaper, particularly that fellow Dustin Fairburn, and keep your wits about you. A murder has been committed, and I fear another may soon transpire if it hasn't already. The very future of the nation may be at stake."

3
Cappuccino Frappuccino Candy Floss

On this late October Saturday afternoon, after returning from their expedition to Kingsmere, Caitlin and Dani were the only customers at Morala's Cup of Java interested in tubs of gelato. Most adults preferred the hot drink that came from a thousand places around the world and seemed to have about a hundred million varieties to order. Chas, the proprietor, peered at the girls oddly when Caitlin asked for a cappuccino frappuccino gelato latte grand petit, while Dani rolled her eyes and ordered "the usual, straight up."

Chas rarely smiled, but now her lips curled when she asked, "You girls know why I keep the gelato counter full, don't you?"

The girls nodded as they both replied, "Thanks."

"Not that I mind keeping an entire counter full of gelato in the fall *and* winter."

"I keep telling you that gelato in the fall and winter will catch on, Chas," Dani said.

"Really?"

"Just call it flavoured Italian snow."

"You could try introducing some new flavours like bubblegum," Caitlin said, "or maybe candy cane, sort of a Christmas special."

"Uh-huh," Chas said, nodding with amusement. "I bet candy floss would be a good bet, too."

"Hey, I should have thought of that," Caitlin said, genuinely disappointed. "Then you could make all coffees with the same flavours so you wouldn't have to worry about getting so many different kinds of beans."

"Why stop there? I could put up a notice that says 'No one over the age of twelve will be admitted.'" Chas pushed the girls' carefully counted change back across the counter. "I don't need your money. Your business advice is payment enough."

"But … but …" both girls stammered.

"Now move along. Someone over twelve would like their bubblegum caffeine. Come back tomorrow. I'll have some more grape gelato then, just in time for winter."

"Cool," Dani said, not noticing Chas's smirk.

The girls wandered down Ottawa's Bank Street, the main thoroughfare in the Glebe. As they strolled, they watched people hurry along to shop. Couples paused outside stores, lingering a little longer than usual in the sunshine to savour the last warmth of an Indian summer. Winter in Ottawa usually came quickly and settled deeply long before the official winter solstice.

"So this strange little Mackenzie King guy," Caitlin said between mouthfuls of gelato, "says we should read Dustin Fairburn's column in the *Glebe Examiner*."

"Right," Dani said, pleased with her friend's grasp of the facts.

"'Cause if we do, we'll get some clues about what Mr. King thinks is so important for us to help him with — you know, murder and stuff like that."

"Right," Dani said, impressed again.

"And then," Caitlin continued, "he'll appear and tell us why all this stuff could change everything in Canada — like our history and our future."

"Right. Makes perfect sense," Dani said, fully satisfied.

"*Hello!* Dani, this is crazy!" Caitlin was so excited that she spat out gelato, the drippings clinging indelicately from her chin.

Dani grinned. "Of course, it seems strange, 'cause this is a mystery and we're detectives again. But this time maybe we get to save Canada. By the way, you've got gelato on your chin."

Caitlin swiped at her face. "And you've got gelato on your overalls."

Dani glanced down but didn't attempt to remove the gelato stains. "Kind of blends in."

"I know you love doing detective stuff, Dani, but we really don't have a clue and Mr. King seems sort of nutty to me."

Dani picked up a copy of the *Glebe Examiner* from a newsstand. "We will, though, and once we gather our clues we'll have a case. And there's no better place to start than Fairburn's column.

Caitlin continued to clean her chin and inspect her clothes as Dani read, re-read, and again read Dustin Fairburn's column. "Wow … amazing … hard to believe."

"Come on, Dani, what the heck does it say?"

"I have no idea."

"Dani!"

Dani continued to scan the article. "Well, there are lots of words, most of 'em pretty big, but I don't know what this stuff has to do with Mr. King. I mean, he was the prime minister of Canada, and Fairburn's article just talks about parks and selling land in Ottawa, which Dustin doesn't seem too happy about. Hey, it even mentions Windsor Park right behind where you live, Caitlin."

"Sell my park? How can anyone sell a park?"

"We could ask Mr. Fairburn," Dani suggested.

"And we'll get a long answer with long words."

"Or we could ask Sadie Squires."

"For an answer that makes sense — to a kid, that is," Caitlin said as Dani began marching off. "Hey! Where are you going?"

"To Abbotsford Home for Senior Citizens just like you said."

Caitlin followed her friend, always a stride behind. "Did you know that when you get wind of a mystery you're as stubborn as Nikki is?"

"Yeah, well, I know someone more stubborn than Nikki and me put together when it comes to winning loonies at cribbage."

"Good point."

Dani put her head down, buried her hands in her overalls, and stretched her lead to two strides. "Mission impossible, but I've got two loonies left and I feel lucky today."

Caitlin sighed heavily. "Poor girl. Poor foolish girl."

Sadie stared down the length of her nose, fixing her gaze through the spectacles perched precariously at the tip. "Now, mind, I could say how it pains an old body to steal loonies from such fine young ladies, but I won't lie to you." Sadie's face creased deeply as she laughed and extended a bony limb to rescue two more coins. "Course, I know my luck can't last forever, and you're both gettin' better — regular cribbage sharks one day soon. So what did you want to ask me, huh?" She whisked the loonies into her dresser drawer and studied her two young friends intently.

Hard to believe she's a hundred years old, Caitlin thought. *In fact, she doesn't look a day over ninety-nine.*

Dani looked at the floor, the walls, the ceiling, everywhere except Sadie. "Um, the thing is —"

Sadie waved a thin arm encouragingly. "I know, child. You can't tell me certain things for certain reasons. I understand. No matter. Just tell me how I can help."

"Thanks, Sadie," Dani said, letting out a huge breath. "I knew we could count on you."

"When you start askin' my advice so you can rob a bank, I might be less cooperative," Sadie said with a wink. "Unless, of course, you cut me in for a third. So what's on your young, eager minds this bright October afternoon?"

Caitlin smiled. "For a third you'd have to drive the getaway car, Sadie."

"Horse and buggy's more my style, child."

Dani frowned impatiently at Caitlin and rolled her eyes. "Sadie, we kind of wondered if you remembered stuff about William Lyon Mackenzie King …"

"Used to be the prime minister of Canada," Caitlin added.

"Thank you, Caitlin," Sadie said. "I might have forgotten that. Course, I remember him. Took us through some tough times — the Great Depression, the Second World War. Never seemed much of a leader somehow, but he outlasted all his critics. Nothin' fancy, bland even, and just between us, bit of an oddball. Oh, it wasn't so much talkin' to ghosts, séances, and such, but it seems he was real stuck on his mother. She was a regular adviser to the PM on world matters, you might say. Mr. King never married. I guess 'cause no one could ever compare to his dearly departed mom.''

Dani stroked her chin thoughtfully. "Sadie, did Mr. King ever have any interest in parks or anything?"

"Parks? Well, since he was the man who created Gatineau Park, I'd have to say, yes, he sure did have an interest in parks."

"Hey, that's where Kingsmere is," Caitlin said.

"Makes sense, don't you think?" Sadie said.

"How about parks in Ottawa, *particularly* ones along the Rideau River?" Dani asked, rising on her toes, something she did whenever she enunciated big words. Then, for emphasis, she tapped her rolled-up *Glebe Examiner*.

"What you got there, child?" Sadie asked.

"Dustin Fairburn's column," Dani answered proudly, spreading the pages dramatically. "He says: 'The City of Ottawa is contemplating selling several pieces of land, including Windsor Park, to developers in order to address its deficit problem, as well as its serious lack of housing.' He also says there's a meeting at City Hall tonight to vote on the Windsor Park sale."

"You don't say?" Sadie said.

"What's a deficit?" Caitlin asked.

"That's when you spend more than you earn," Sadie answered. "But that's no excuse for sellin' parks. The fools! What in the world, though, has all that got to do with our long-deceased prime minister?"

Both girls shrugged.

"We were hoping you'd know," Dani finally said.

Sadie blinked several times. "Much as I love you girls, you do tax an old body's mind. How could a much-dead PM have anything to do with a present group of money-grubbin' —" She stopped speaking suddenly when she noticed the wary expressions on the two girls' faces. "All right, I know I'm not supposed to go there. I did say I wouldn't ask too many questions about your latest adventure."

The girls grinned as Sadie checked the big dial on her men's wristwatch. "'Sides, it's time for my afternoon game of cribbage with Eunice." She leaned forward and whispered, "Poor thing's memory is going. Feel real sorry for the old girl, but not enough to let her win, mind. Cribbage is good for keepin' the mind's movin' parts all workin'. So when's our next game, girls?"

"I think we'll have to wait until we're paid our allowance." Dani said. "How 'bout next Saturday?"

"It's a date," Sadie said, waving a bony finger. "Don't forget."

"We won't," Caitlin said.

"We've got a bit to learn yet," Dani offered.

Sadie chuckled. "And when you've learned all there is to know, you can come and take back all them loonies I'm holdin' for you."

"It's a deal," Dani said.

Sadie's smile faded as she wrapped an arm around each girl. "Don't know what in tarnation you two are up to this time, but be careful, for the sake of these old bones, will you?"

"We will," Caitlin promised.

"Besides, what trouble could *we* get into?" Dani added.

The three friends paused for several seconds to consider Dani's words, then erupted into laughter.

"No more than a pack of beagles in a bagel shop," Sadie concluded.

4
The Politics of Parks

Dani's dad, John, stood first on one leg, then the other as he peered over the crowd. "There's Mayor Perkins and Dustin Fairburn. And, look, here comes Jim Watson, the former mayor. Gosh, girls, standing room only in City Hall tonight. I think it's great you two are taking an active interest in local politics and your community."

"Parks, Dad. We're interested in parks."

"Right."

"Order, order!" Mayor Perkins commanded, banging his wooden gavel long after the crowd's murmuring had faded to silence. When the last bang echoed loudly, the mayor looked briefly embarrassed before speaking. "Well, we have an important vote before us this evening that has to be decided quickly. And since we've got an unusually large crowd tonight in the civic chamber, we'd better get started." The mayor tapped the gavel on his palm almost challengingly.

John leaned down and whispered, "That's what you call passive-aggressive behaviour, girls."

"Except for the passive part, I think you're right, Dad," Dani whispered back.

"I'd call the mayor's behaviour aggressive-aggressive," Caitlin, too, whispered.

Dani and her dad hissed, *"Shh!"* and attracted the attention of the entire gathering of concerned citizens.

"Now we have this Windsor Park land development motion before council today," the mayor said, "and lots of folks here have all kinds of feelings about it this way and that."

Before the mayor could say anything further, a group of citizens unravelled a banner and began to chant, "You CAD you, you CAD you." The banner said: CAD — CITIZENS AGAINST DEVELOPMENT.

Fuming, the mayor turned seven shades of red before pounding his gavel again. "Silence! Order! Silence!"

Then Jim Watson's deep voice cut through the mob. "Your Worship, these people have the right to express their opposition to this motion. As spokesperson for CAD —"

The mayor glared. "I know who you are and why you're here, sir. Let me just say there's a big difference between expressing opinions and disrupting council meetings. What's more, the time for meaningless protest has passed. Besides, I was about to make an announcement before I was interrupted by your hooligans, Mr. *Former* Mayor."

An anonymous voice floated over the crowd, shouting, "Jim Watson for mayor!"

While a number of other people hooted and laughed, veins bulged in Mayor Perkins's neck as he said through clenched teeth, "The last council meeting ended in a tie vote regarding the land development motion. I asked council members then to reconsider and vote again, at a later date, on the proposal from the Mitchell Development Company to build ninety-eight townhouses on the land adjacent to the Rideau River in what is currently called Windsor Park. I advised my esteemed fellow councillors to vote in favour of the motion in view of the many obvious financial benefits to our city, especially at a time when we desperately need to cut our deficit and alleviate our current housing crisis. I now urge council members to reassess their municipal responsibility and vote accordingly tonight. However, first I must regrettably make an announcement."

Silence descended on the crowd, and the mayor relaxed his grip on the gavel, enjoying full control of the boisterous crowd.

"It is with great sadness that I announce that Councillor Gertrude Owens was found dead this morning."

Gasps and cries filled the civic chamber.

"What?"

"How?"

"When?"

The mayor held up a hand and slammed his gavel to still the crowd. "Such questions aren't appropriate to this meeting. Funeral arrangements will be made public tomorrow. As you know, Councillor Owens was an outspoken opponent of the motion before us, but I don't think we can afford to let emotion cloud our judgment on such a critical issue. So, without further adieu, members of council, please raise your hands if you support the motion to allow Mitchell Development to build townhouses in Windsor Park." The mayor counted quickly, and a half-smile attached itself to the side of his mouth as he asked, "Opposed?" He counted again. "Twelve in favour, eleven opposed. Therefore, the sale of Windsor Park to Mitchell Development will proceed as proposed. The motion is carried. Now, with fourteen million dollars more soon to be in the civic coffers, I gratefully move to the next item on our agenda."

As the mayor continued with other issues, stunned and suddenly silent members of the crowd began to exit the civic chamber.

"What does this mean, Dad?" Dani asked.

"It means that by next spring Caitlin's family will have ninety-eight townhouses in their backyard."

"But, Dad, how could such a dumb thing be decided in five minutes? No one even got to speak."

"It's because that councillor died, isn't it?" Caitlin said, tears in her eyes.

"I'm afraid so," John said. "The public had its chance months ago. This was the final vote. Councillor Owens's sudden death broke the deadlock and allowed the mayor's side to win.

"Isn't there anything we can do, Dad?"

"No, I'm afraid not," John said, scratching his forehead and standing on one leg. "Democracy requires that we respect the majority, even if we don't agree with it."

"But, Dad, most people don't want this, even if those councillors and the mayor think so."

"Well, I'm sorry, girls, but the voters elected them to repre-sent our interests. Look, there's a washroom. Be right back."

Caitlin sniffed. "Doesn't seem right."

"Caitlin, the councillor's *dead* — remember what Mr. King said? We have to watch and listen for clues."

"How in the world can we find out anything, Dani? And even if we could, it wouldn't change the vote. Remember, she's *dead*!"

"Don't you see, Caitlin? Maybe she was murdered, just like the person Mr. King was talking about at Kingsmere! This must have something to do with what he was telling us."

"How in the world could building townhouses in a park, which hasn't even happened yet, have anything to do with a dead prime minister and murder?"

"It's a mystery," Dani said, stroking her chin. "All I know is that Mr. King has been a ghost for an awful long time and an awful lot of people don't want this development to happen …"

The girls heard a toilet flush inside the men's washroom.

"And we don't want all their efforts to go down the toilet," Caitlin added.

The girls grinned at each other as John opened the washroom door.

"Oh, I see we're *all* feeling some relief," John said, clearly clueless about why the girls were smiling.

5
A Mother's Wish

"Your dad sure looked happy when you said you might be interested in looking at cottages in the Gatineau," Caitlin said as she ate some pumpkin pie.

"I had to say I was interested," Dani said, wolfing down her own pumpkin pie. "Otherwise how would we have gotten him to drop us off at Kingsmere while he looked at a few hundred more?" Dani frowned. "Caitlin, why are you pointing to your nose?"

"I'm trying to show you where the whipped cream is on your face."

Dani swiped at her nose, managing to spread whipped cream across both nostrils. "We need to get information from Mr. King, especially about the murder he mentioned." She placed both elbows on the table. "He wants us to help him solve a murder, but he hasn't given us any of the facts."

"And if we help him," Caitlin said, pointing to her nose again, "maybe he can help us get rid of those land developers."

"Exactly what I had in mind, Watson," Dani said, ignoring Caitlin, who was still pointing at her nose.

"Thank you, Sherlock."

Dani wrinkled her whipped-cream nose. "And I'd bet a crate of gelato that one of the murder victims is Councillor Owens, but who's the other one?"

"Honestly, Dani, we don't know what really happened to Councillor Owens. You can't jump to conclusions like that."

"You've got to admit it's pretty suspicious, though."

Caitlin furrowed her brow. "I suppose …"

The girls were conducting their discussion of recent events in the Moorside Tearoom on Sunday morning. Tourists had lined up for tea and dessert after an excursion through October leaves. Joining the ghost tour not long before Halloween was an autumn ritual for many people.

"Dani, you've got whipped cream on your nose," a ghostly voice commented.

Dani gulped down an unusually large mouthful of pie, and Caitlin sprayed the table with the remainder of her semi-chewed piece.

"Yes, quite. A waste of food, to be sure. But the pie here now doesn't compare to the creations my housekeeper, Mrs. Lansdowne, used to make me for me when this tearoom was my cottage." King had materialized in the chair next to the girls, which a moment earlier had been unoccupied. "Sorry, young ladies, I've been nearby all along and didn't anticipate the effect my sudden appearance might have on you."

Caitlin wiped pie from the contorted expression on her face and placed the napkin on her plate. "Mr. King, do you mean you always live at Kingsmere?"

A slight smile formed on the former prime minister's lips. "Living isn't what I do much of anymore. Actually, not at all. But if you're asking if I reside here, then, yes, I do and have been doing so in these forests and meadows since I died over there of pneumonia at the Farm in 1950."

Dani stroked her chin and smeared more pie there. "Why do you have to stay here, Mr. King? My dad says you were buried in Toronto."

The former prime minister's eyes nervously surveyed the bustling tearoom. Great bellows of laughter erupted from a distant table. Closer by, fragments of conversation could be overheard.

"A McDonald's would speed things up here."

"And it would be cheaper, too."

"I wonder if anyone ever thought about putting a Tim Hortons in here?"

King puffed out his chest and fumbled with his pocket watch. "Nincompoops. Bigger crowds and modern food factories — original thought, indeed! My dear friends, if I may call you that, please join me for a stroll of Kingsmere so I can explain why I'm still here more than fifty years after my death."

The girls carefully counted their change, paid quickly, and watched as their table was pounced on by waiting graduates of a recent ghost tour.

"My dear mother would be appalled at such atrocious manners," King muttered, glaring at the table pouncers.

As the trio stepped outside, they were greeted by a cold October wind. The girls immediately zipped up their coats.

"Mr. King," Caitlin said with concern, "if you don't wear something warmer, you'll catch a death of a cold."

Dani rolled her eyes as King warmed to the girls. "It's a pity I can't catch a cold so that I could sneeze on some of those tourists. Sorry, girls, I find myself increasingly annoyed at such spectacles. Why if I was prime minister today, I'd … I'd …" King sighed. "I'd probably dither, delay, and do nothing."

The girls arched their brows. "Huh?"

"Oh, yes, today I feel within myself the desire, the wherewithal, if not the courage, to act, but then I —"

Dani bent to pick up a fallen pinecone. "That's all very interesting, sir, but what does it have to do with murder?"

King ignored Dani's question. He walked with a worried expression, his hands clasped behind his back. "I've been here in spirit all these many years because I couldn't act decisively as prime minister or in my private life."

"How come?" Caitlin asked.

As the trio arrived at the edge of the lake, steps below Kingswood Cottage, King continued speaking without replying to Caitlin's question. "I've spent countless hours gazing across the water from this spot, and the view has never ceased to move me." Suddenly, King turned to the girls, agitated and half mumbling. "Oh, yes, I was prime minister longer than anyone else in Canada or in the Commonwealth — a good twenty-two years. I led our people through the Great Depression, the Second World War — a war we very nearly lost. I helped found the United Nations, set up our first national unemployment insurance, laid the groundwork for Newfoundland and Labrador to join Confederation, and made Canada truly independent of Britain. When I left office, this nation was on the threshold of its greatest period of prosperity. But, alas, I was still a failure."

"Mr. King, sir, I'm afraid you're not making much sense," Dani said. "If you did all those things, how could you be a failure? And besides, my dad says you're on the fifty-dollar bill."

The former prime minister glowered. "And how often do you see a fifty-dollar bill, Dani?"

"I've never seen one."

"Me, neither," Caitlin piped up.

"Exactly my point! You see, girls, people in this country keep me out of sight and out of mind. I was the master of obfuscation and obstruction, never doing things by half if I could manage by quarters. Governing as such served my purpose."

"What purpose was that?" Caitlin asked.

"To keep my political opponents off balance so I could evade issues and retain power. In my private life I was equally indecisive. I once loved, and might have again, but my mother advised both in life and in death that I remain unattached. I didn't want to displease Mother, but, oh, how I regret taking her counsel in the affairs of the heart."

"So why did you?" Caitlin prodded.

"Because my mother insisted there wasn't a woman on this earth who was good enough for me, who could replace her …"

Dani fiddled with her pinecone. "Mr. King, you promised to tell us about the murder, and now it's real important 'cause we think another murder might have already happened. Yesterday Gertrude Owens, an Ottawa city councillor, died, and she was going to vote against selling Windsor Park in Ottawa."

King's eyes lit up. "Ah, strange, especially that we should be talking here at the very place where the first murder was committed." He poked a pile of leaves with his walking stick. "Two deaths, seemingly unrelated, except that both victims had the deciding vote concerning the sale of land to developers. To some these two deaths might seem coincidental, but we in the spirit world know that such apparent coincidences often mask a design or purpose far from coincidental."

"Both of the murdered people had deciding votes on the sale of land?" Dani cried.

"Yes, indeed," King said, a little annoyed at the interruption. "The man murdered at Kingsmere that I spoke of earlier was a fellow named Guy Williams, who was on the National Capital Commission's board of directors. He intended to vote against selling a large parcel of land adjacent to Kingsmere and just outside Gatineau Park."

"More townhouses!" Caitlin yelped.

King scowled, then let a slight smile curl his lips. "Indubitably. No foul play has been suspected in either death. But, mark my words, both were murdered by the same despicable hand — a hand that offered a cup of tea last Friday evening to Mr. Williams, the better to enjoy the wondrous late-night air of this estate. Each victim, I am certain, was killed by a slow-acting poison concealed in an offered refreshment. To the unwary, a heart attack would seem to be the culprit."

"But who was the killer?" Dani asked, her eyes wide.

King sighed. "Alas, I never got a good look at the villain."

Caitlin frowned. "But how did you know who the murdered man was?"

"I recognized his face in the newspaper the next day when it was reported that Mr. Guy Williams died of an apparent heart attack while driving his automobile late Friday night."

The girls looked across the water, half expecting to glimpse an unsettling image or two, then glanced away, afraid to see or hear anything more. A sudden wind carried a swirl of blood-coloured leaves from the spot of the murder up and away across Kingsmere Lake.

King broke the long silence as the girls shivered. "This view of my beloved lake, like those who accepted death disguised in a drink, has been poisoned forever."

6

The Three Musketeers

"Poisoned?" Dani repeated for the zillionth time.

King, Dani, and Caitlin were back in the tearoom, where the girls were enjoying another helping of pumpkin pie.

"Mr. King," Dani said, "this stuff's real interesting. I mean sad and kind of interesting. And I guess you know we like mysteries, but Councillor Owens is already dead, the vote for the sale of Windsor Park has already happened, and now you tell us a guy named Williams is dead, too, and that some land next to Kingsmere's about to be gobbled up by townhouses. What the heck can we do about all of that?"

"We *are* only twelve, you know," Caitlin added.

King nodded sagely. "What to do, yes. What can anyone do? No one to ask advice from, confide in all these years …"

"It's okay," Caitlin said soothingly. "We can listen and you can confide in us."

"We do have some detective experience, Mr. King," Dani assured him. "And with your help, who knows, maybe we can be like the three musketeers and solve these murders."

King wiped his moist eyes and cleared his throat. "Yes, that's right, the three of us … musketeers. Oh, girls, you have no idea how much that thought warms my cold heart."

"Did you say musketeers or mouseketeers?" Caitlin asked.

Dani rolled her eyes. "Musketeers are from the old days, like when Mr. King was young."

"Yes, well, indeed when I was young, I was best friends and shared living quarters with Bert Harper and Henry Burbidge, and together we fashioned ourselves as three musketeers, though not quite the original authentic version of that great French novelist Alexandre Dumas. But, oh, my, we were inseparable and it was a wonderful time. In fact, it was with Bert that I first discovered Kingsmere so long ago. Bert and I were young, full of ambition, and we saw ourselves as men of destiny but, alas, it didn't last. I looked up to Bert, yes, even envied his confidence, his decisiveness. He seemed indestructible, and so it was an utter shock when we learned he had drowned."

"Drowned?" the girls echoed.

"Yes," King said quietly. "He drowned in the Ottawa River in 1901 selflessly trying to save Bessie Blair who had fallen through thin ice during a skating party. She was the daughter of the minister of railways and canals."

"That's terrible!" Caitlin said through a well-chewed braid.

King furiously rubbed his hands together as if he intended to start a fire in his palms. "Yes, my best true friend, my hero, acted without a thought for his own safety and tried to save Bessie's life but, sadly, they both perished." King looked across the room as if he could see all the way to the Ottawa River, then mumbled, "'If I lose myself, I save myself.'"

"Huh?" both girls said.

"I'm quoting from the inscription on dear Bert's statue near Parliament Hill, attesting to his gallant courage in the face of adversity. His will to act was a quality that unfortunately I always lacked."

"What do you mean, Mr. King?" Dani asked.

"I dithered and delayed and as such managed to become Canada's longest-serving prime minister. I couldn't lose myself and therefore didn't save myself."

"Until now," Dani said decisively.

"Pardon me?" King asked, confused and blinking.

Caitlin spat out her braid and said with excitement, "Yeah, Mr. King, 'cause now you have us and together we're three musketeers. Isn't that right, Dani?"

"Absolutely." Dani turned and nodded at her friend. "Together, somehow, we can all act."

"The three musketeers," Mr. King muttered. Then he straightened himself, rising to his full height, which wasn't much. "My dear friends, would you do me the honour of calling me Rex?"

"Hey, Rex, just like a dog," Caitlin burbled with excitement, then looked embarrassed.

"I should be so honoured to be compared to the noble dog, but I got the nickname in university," King said, chuckling. "You see, *rex* is Latin for *king*."

"It still sounds like a dog's name to me," Caitlin said. "What do you think, Pat?" She bent down to pet King's phantom pooch.

As she stroked the air, a voice suddenly said, "Hey, Caitlin, what are you doing?"

Both girls jumped.

"I was practising petting Nicki," Caitlin said hurriedly

to John, Dani's dad, who had appeared in the tearoom seemingly out of nowhere.

"'Cause he likes to be petted in a certain way," Dani added unconvincingly.

"Huh?" John said with true confusion. "You could pet Nicki with a ten-foot pole and he wouldn't know the difference between that and a trained dog massage therapist."

"Huh?" Dani and Caitlin said with even truer confusion.

"Doesn't matter," John said. "But what does matter is that I've found the old O'Neill Farm, our ancestral home. And guess what? It's close to Mackenzie King Estate, just outside Gatineau Park. And it's now owned by the National Capital Commission, too. Come on, I'll show you."

"I thought you were looking at cottages, Dad," Dani said.

"I know, but before we came up here again I went to Library and Archives Canada on the Web to check on the whereabouts of the O'Neill Farm, something I've always meant to do. I knew it was somewhere around here, but just didn't know exactly where. Now I've solved the mystery."

Dani smiled, thinking about their own mystery. "Good thinking, Dad."

"I know what your father is talking about, girls," King said. "The farm he speaks of is quite close. I'll go with you and will be right behind you."

"Okay," Caitlin whispered, "we'll lead the way."

"You don't have to whisper, Caitlin," Dani whispered back. "Dad can't hear Rex."

John looked puzzled. "You lead the way? Can't hear? You're pulling my leg, girls. I'll lead the way, since I know where the farm is, and remember, I can hear everything."

"If only the poor chap knew the truth," King said, falling in line behind the girls. "I daresay this confusion between what you can see and hear and what your poor parent can't is rather fun, don't you think?"

"Don't you feel sorry for Dani's dad, Rex?" Caitlin asked.

"Oh, pardon me. I didn't mean any disrespect …"

Caitlin grinned. "I'm just joking, Rex."

"Oh, dear, I've always been such a stick in the mud. I don't even understand humour, let alone know how to tell a proper joke."

"I don't think jokes are supposed to be proper, Rex," Caitlin said. "But I'm sure we can help you tell a funny joke."

The girls began marching behind John.

"That's the spirit," John said.

"No, actually I'm the spirit," King piped up.

The girls laughed.

"Now that's a real joke," Caitlin said.

"Give me a high-five," Dani said.

John turned and slowed his eager pace. He watched the girls laugh, exchange high-fives with each other, then do the same thing with the air. "What's so funny? I just can't see it."

"You can say that again," King said.

The girls almost fell over laughing, then pulled themselves together and resumed marching.

John sighed and muttered to himself, "And I was afraid they wouldn't want to come along."

7
Punishment for Trespassers

"Dad? Hey, Dad!" Dani shouted for the third time.

John stared across the meadow without speaking, lost in thought.

"Dad, there's a bear behind you! Dad, the bear's going to jump on your back!" *Time for desperate measures,* Dani thought, stroking her chin.

"Tell him you're dying to go look at more cottages," Caitlin suggested. "Speaking of dying, why did Rex disappear back there?"

"You know, it's very strange," John began slowly, "and you might start to think I'm a bit weird …"

"Dad, it's too late to start thinking that," Dani said.

"I've run and skied near here for years but didn't know the old family farm was so close. And now that I know and we're actually here, well, I have this strange feeling, like I know this place. It speaks to me from some long-forgotten past."

Dani noticed that her dad's eyes were moist. "How do you mean?"

"I can't explain really, but it's like something or someone is waiting for me here."

"Maybe there is, Dad."

"Nah, couldn't be."

"Hey, you people there! You're trespassin'!" A cranky-looking old man stalked toward the girls and John with furious, shaky strides, while a much larger, much younger man lumbered behind timidly. The old man halted and parked himself a few centimetres in front of John's face. The young man, staring at his oversized feet, failed to notice that the old man had stopped, and bumped into his back. The old man was pushed forward so that it seemed as if he and John were kissing before both men pushed away from each other in a hurry.

The girls couldn't help giggling as the old man turned to the young giant and snarled, "You clumsy fool!"

Goliath didn't speak. Instead he backed up as he surveyed everyone else with a worried frown.

The old man shook his head and growled something under his breath, then faced John with an accusing finger all the while using the fingers of his other hand to rake furiously through his dishevelled white hair. The girls watched with fascination as tiny flakes of dandruff drifted through shafts of sunlight and landed on his and John's clothes. John brushed at the clinging flakes in horror as the older man continued to scratch.

"Don't know if you saw the sign or not, but I'm tellin' you now straight out," the old man bellowed. "You're on private property."

John cringed as another cloud of flakes blew his way.

"Private property? This isn't private property. I've been told it belongs to the National Capital Commission."

The older man snorted. "Did belong, you mean. I suppose you read the papers about as well as you read private property signs."

"Now ... now look here," John sputtered, "this is public property and I don't have to explain to you why we're here."

The old man turned to the sheepish colossus behind him. "Just like I told you, Double J, the great unwashed and unread public won't stay away from my property until we put that fence up. Didn't I tell you that, boy?"

The young man's perpetual state of shyness was only heightened by the old man's question. He placed his index finger alongside his face and contemplated his shoes.

Wow! Dani thought. *They're as big as canoes!*

Bet this guy could snowboard without a board, Caitlin thought.

"It's like talkin' to a doorknob," the old man muttered before turning back to John.

"Fence?" John said. "You can't put a fence up here. Are you crazy?"

"Crazy?" The old man scratched his head harder. "Yeah, I've been called crazy before and a whole bunch of other things, but I've had the last laugh with every million I've made."

So he can *afford dandruff shampoo,* Caitlin thought.

John stood on one leg, then the other. "And what the devil does that have to do with putting up a fence on land owned by the Canadian public?"

"Ha!" the old man spat out. "Just this." His fingers scattered dandruff flakes all over John's black leather coat. "The Mitchell Development Company — that's me — is buildin' a hundred and fifty townhouses on this property.

By this time next year they'll all be just about built. When that happens, you tell all those proud homeowners they're on public property. See how they like it."

A muscle in John's face twitched while a vein in his neck bulged. "You have no right. I have more of a stake here than you ever could. This … this was once my grandfather's farm."

"Everybody's property was once somebody else's. Things change. It's the way of the world, don't you know?" The ornery old man glanced at the gentle giant. "This boy here ain't gonna mope around after his granddad's property, are you, boy?"

Eyes zeroed in on the speechless young man. "Yes, sir. No, sir. I don't know." The giant's meaty fingers covered his face and mouth, obscuring most of what he had said.

"I take it back. My grandson's not a doorknob. He's a fence post. And that's why he and his nitwit friend are gonna build a big fence around this useless meadow."

John's bulgy eyes betrayed shock and anger at the thought of his newly rediscovered homestead being trampled on, torn up, and kicked around. His lips barely formed the words *useless meadow* before the old man continued.

"Useless, that is, until I build my townhouses. Dim-witted, dirt-poor Irish farmers never made a penny farmin' these rocks and trees, but I'm gonna make millions." The ancient geezer gestured as if shooing away flies. "Now, folks, if you'll excuse us, recess is over. Time to move on."

As the old guy turned and shepherded his gargantuan grandson away, John struggled with a rebuttal. His mouth opened and closed like a fish's, but words didn't emerge.

Suddenly, the old curmudgeon thought of something, half turned, and said over his shoulder, "Oh, yeah, another reason why you should leave is that when we came up the path we saw a bear with her cub. You don't want those girls of yours to be lunch for a couple of hungry beasts, do you?"

While John stood frozen, Dani blurted out, "Say, mister, how fast can *you* run?"

The old man puffed out his narrow chest as his grandson hung off to the side, trying to avoid eye contact. "Don't you know you can't outrun a bear?"

Dani hooked her hands in her overall straps. "Oh, I wasn't thinking of outrunning any bears. We just need to make sure we can outrun *you*."

"Huh? Whaddaya mean by that?" the geezer shouted.

"Come on, Dad," Dani said. "I think we're safe from bears."

As they walked away, Caitlin looked over her shoulder and saw the old man still puzzling and scratching while his grandson continued to inspect the leaf-littered ground.

John now had a grin splashed across his face. Finally, he managed to croak, "Well, that was … I mean, we really … that is, you …"

"Come on, Dad. We've got work to do."

"We do?"

"Of course we do! We have to find a way to stop that guy from ruining this park."

"And our family farm," John said morosely. "Guess it's time to call a lawyer."

"Guess it's time to think of a plan."

"Guess it's time for gelato," Caitlin said. "I can't bear another minute without it."

8
The Mystery of Adolescence

"You'll just have to grin and bear it," Dani said to Kathleen, her upset sister.

"I have no intention of bearing this boredom for long and we have no intention of grinning about anything, right, Samantha?" Kathleen retorted, glaring for emphasis.

"I wouldn't grin for a million dollars," Caitlin's sister, Samantha, agreed, icicles hanging from every word.

"Surely, Dad could've looked for cottages on the Internet before dragging us all out into the wilderness," Kathleen complained.

"Who knows? Maybe something exciting will happen," Caitlin said, shrugging as she returned her attention to her waffle cone of gelato.

"You never know," Dani agreed.

"These children obviously believe in fairy tales," Kathleen said.

"Obviously," Samantha said.

Dani and Caitlin smiled at each other, then chimed, "Obviously."

The four girls stood outside the land registry office in the town of Wakefield, Quebec, waiting for Dani's dad. He had bribed the four girls into coming on yet another weekend cottage-hunting autumn expedition with the promise of all the gelato they could eat. But on the ride up the elder girls had read an article on dieting and decided to pass on fattening foods. Dani had set a new world record for speedy gelato consumption, and only Caitlin still slowly slurped her maple-flavoured Italian ice.

"This was a silly idea," Kathleen said indignantly.

"When I think of what else we —" Samantha started to say.

"This is terrible!" John almost yelled as he walked toward the girls at breakneck speed.

"I can't bear to hear," Caitlin whispered.

"Are you sure you want to be the bearer of bad news, Dad?" Dani quipped, delighted she had thought up yet another sentence with *bear* in it.

"Dad, can we go home now?" Kathleen whined with impatience, "You're not making much sense, and Samantha and I have very important —"

"But I've got terrible news! The Mitchell Development Company really does legally own the old O'Neill farmland."

"Dad, you didn't even know where the O'Neill Farm was a few days ago," Kathleen reasoned.

John's eyes had a funny, moist glaze. "I know, I know …"

Dani slammed her fist into her hand. "Ouch! We've got to do something. Right, Caitlin?"

"Dani," Caitlin said around her last mouthful of gelato,

"is that the big shy teenager who's building a fence around the old farm?"

Two teenagers moved along the bend of the Gatineau River toward the girls and John. The larger of the two trailed behind the smaller boy, who bounced on the balls of his feet with abundant energy. Every few strides the smaller teen turned to his giant friend and announced a new marvel of the day: sparkling river water, crisp October air, newly fallen leaves. The larger teen nodded but didn't speak.

"I think you're right," Dani said, "and they're headed this way."

Slowly, the larger teenager ambled toward Wakefield General Store, while his smaller companion talked and walked circles around him.

When Nikki howled, Caitlin thought, *Those boys look like a Chihuahua running circles around a St. Bernard.*

As the two teens arrived at the general store, the larger one shyly glanced up from his shoes and said, "Sorry we have to build that fence over at the farm."

Several moments passed before anyone had the presence of mind to respond, then Dani asked, "Have you built a fence around the entire property yet?"

"It's what we're doing now," the huge teenager said, avoiding eye contact.

"Do you mean to say, young man," John interjected, stepping forward, "you don't think there should be a fence there?"

The big teenager's eyes shifted nervously, but it was the smaller boy who spoke first. "Nah, Double J and I don't like putting up the fence at all. We think it's a crime. It's owned by the NCC, right? And that's the government, right? And, anyway, it's hard work, right? That's why Double J and I are taking a break and getting some snacks."

"I'd rather be reading a good book," Double J said.

"You like reading books?" Kathleen asked, a glint in her eye.

Double J's own eyes lit up. "Yes, I really do. I want to major in English literature when I go to university. I love reading."

Samantha leaned forward. "Who are your favourite writers?"

Double J grinned. "At the moment Tolkien, Tolstoy, Twain … I'm working my way through the T's."

"Don't forget William Makepeace Thackeray," the smaller teen added.

"Samantha and I just finished reading *Vanity Fair* for our book club," Kathleen gushed.

Dani and Caitlin both rolled their eyes and snorted.

"Double J and I have been thinking of starting our own book club," the smaller boy said.

"Maybe we could start a book club with you two," Double J said boldly, looking hopefully at Kathleen and Samantha.

An awkward, though not unpleasant, silence followed as the four teenagers alternately grinned, blushed, and scraped their feet. The smaller boy was about to list his top fifty books when John loudly cleared his throat with the intention of speaking.

"Now let me get this straight. You're building a fence around the old O'Neill Farm but would rather be reading and you don't agree, that is, you and your friend here —"

"My name's Pete, but people call me Pipsqueak," the smaller teen interrupted, holding out his hand to John. "And my friend here is Double J, because his dad was Junior, so he'd be Junior Junior if we didn't call him Double J. As for building the fence, Old Man Mitchell tricked us. We made a deal with him, and now we're stuck with it."

"How did he trick you?" Kathleen asked.

"And who's Old Man Mitchell?" Samantha demanded.

"Double J's grumpy grandfather, of course," Pipsqueak replied. "He tricked us into working for the whole year doing whatever needs doing. He said he'd pay us double or nothing."

Five mouths verbalized a single syllable: "Huh?"

"Double or nothing," Pipsqueak repeated, bobbing in and out, up and down like a nervous rooster. "Old Man Mitchell said we were weaklings and couldn't last a year doing manual work the way he did when he was half our age. Then he made Double J mad. Real mad. Old Man Mitchell said Double J was weak just like Double J's dad, who's dead. The ornery old guy said Double J would probably end up worthless, too."

"He didn't!" Samantha cried.

"He couldn't!" Kathleen yelped.

"He did and he could!" Pipsqueak affirmed. "And then Double J's grandfather made us a bet. If we worked for a year and never asked questions about what he told us to do, he'd give us double our pay for university. But if we quit working or asked even one question, we'd get nothing for the entire year. Nothing at all."

"He didn't!" Kathleen yelped.

"He couldn't!" Samantha cried.

"He did and he could!" Pete confirmed.

"We've worked almost ten months now," Double J said to no one in particular, all the while staring at his mammoth feet.

"So we practise, Double J and I, when we're working," Pipsqueak continued. "We ask each other questions like,

'Why are we building a fence on land that should be part of the park?' That way we don't end up asking Old Man Mitchell why we're doing what we're doing."

"Seems sensible," John said. "I can appreciate your dilemma, and I don't blame you boys personally for putting up that fence around my family's farm …"

"We're real sorry about that, sir," Double J said.

"I know you are."

"But why is Double J's grandfather so mean?" Caitlin asked.

"That's one of the questions we keep asking each other while we're working," Pipsqueak said. "Poor Double J has had to put up with Old Man Mitchell his entire life."

"He hasn't!" Samantha gasped.

"He couldn't!" Kathleen gasp.

"He has and he could!" Dani and Caitlin shouted with more than a trace of exasperation.

"Well, we better get some snacks and scoot back to building the fence or else Old Man Mitchell will say we've broken our agreement and he doesn't have to pay us."

"He —" Kathleen and Samantha said together, then stopped short when they noticed Dani and Caitlin glaring at them.

"That grouchy old man watches us like a hawk," Pipsqueak said dejectedly, kicking at the gravel on the shoulder of the road. Then he suddenly cheered up and beamed at Samantha. "Maybe Double J and I could meet you and Kathleen somewhere and talk about setting up our own book club…. I mean, if your father doesn't mind …"

Samantha and Kathleen blushed appropriately, nodded, and glanced at John.

"I guess there wouldn't be any harm in that," John said.

"I can only speak for Kathleen, though. But I'll check with Bob, Samantha's father, and see what he thinks."

"Maybe if Samantha, Double J, Pipsqueak, and I put our heads together we can figure out how to convince Double J's grandfather to stop what he's doing to the old O'Neill Farm," Kathleen said in her most wheedling voice.

"That's right," Samantha said. "Four heads are better than one."

"I'm sure Bob won't have a problem with Samantha being part of your think tank," John said, smiling.

Dani tapped Caitlin on the shoulder and whispered, "Hey, if we don't watch out, our sisters will be doing all the detective work. We'd better do something fast!"

"Like what?"

"I don't know yet, but something will come to me," Dani said, stroking her chin. "It always does."

Caitlin groaned. "Detective Dani, do you think Double J's grandfather murdered Councillor Owens and that Williams guy?"

"Double J's grandfather is starting to look as guilty as Nikki does after stealing food from the kitchen table."

"So we have two mysteries to solve," Caitlin said.

"You mean two murders."

Caitlin shook her head. "I didn't say two murders. I said two mysteries."

"Are you talking about Mr. King and the mystery of why his country seems to ignore him?"

"Huh?"

"Well, if it isn't that, what in howling beagles *is* the second mystery?"

"The mystery of our elder, wiser sisters actually having boyfriends."

Dani scrunched up her face as if Caitlin had suggested she eat worms. "Yuck. I don't think I want to go there. I'd rather tackle something a whole lot easier — like murder."

"So, Sherlock, what next?"

"We're going to have to look for clues."

"No kidding, but how?"

"I haven't a clue."

"Great! Then maybe we'd better get cracking."

Dani stroked her chin. "I've got it!"

"What?"

"I know just what I need to dream up a detective plan."

"Darn it, Dani! What?"

"Dad, oh, Dad, can Caitlin and I have more gelato?"

9
Politics Made Easy

"I don't know why I didn't think about this earlier," Dani said, standing on tiptoe and pulling on her overall straps as the doorbell to the entrance of the Victorian mansion rang out. "Dustin Fairburn knows everything about history and politics and stuff. Once we ask about the land development — of course, we can't say anything about the murders — he'll tell us exactly what we need to do to convince the city council, the NCC, and everyone else to leave Windsor Park and my family's farm alone. And once everybody finds out what's been happening and that beautiful parkland could be lost forever, then they'll just vote to keep things the way they are. Don't you think so, Caitlin?"

"I certainly hope so," Caitlin said, concern creasing her face.

"Don't worry, Caitlin. Just leave everything to me."

The heavy wooden door slowly opened, and a rumpled, unsmiling man blinked at the girls over reading glasses.

"Hello, Professor Fairburn," Dani said. "Remember us?"

"Ah, yes, the girl detectives."

"Guess you weren't expecting us," Dani said, zeroing in on the obvious.

"To be sure, I wasn't, and I'm rather busy at the moment with an academic paper and an unforgiving deadline …"

"Well, then, we won't take up much of your time 'cause we know how important your work is to the university and we wouldn't want the old place to shut down because of us. We read your column against ruining Caitlin's park, I mean, Windsor Park, with townhouses and stuff. So, actually, we only have one small question and, well, I guess I'll come straight to the point."

The professor rubbed his ever-wrinkling forehead. "Please do."

"How can you change something that hasn't happened yet but which politicians have decided will happen, even though all the people don't want it to happen?"

Fairburn placed two fingers on the bridge of his nose but didn't speak. Caitlin thought, *That's what my dad does when Mom talks about taking yoga. Says it gives him a migraine, whatever that is.*

When the professor still remained silent, Dani forged on. "What I mean, sir, is, like, selling the park because the politicians are spending more money than they're earning."

Fairburn took a deep breath and sighed. "You mean because of the city deficit.

Dani grinned. "That's it!"

"I'm afraid the political process is quite complex and can be difficult to comprehend without years of academic rigour. Even those with experience and the necessary credentials often don't have adequate answers."

"To my question, you mean?" Dani said.

"Precisely." Fairburn glanced at his watch as Dani's face scrunched up for the next question.

"But, sir, all I'm asking is how the heck do politics work so that people get the stuff they want?"

"'Cause we live in a democracy," Caitlin added.

"Yeah, that's right," Dani said, nodding. "Isn't a democracy supposed to get people what they voted for?"

Here comes that migraine thing again, Caitlin thought, watching the professor stroke his nose.

Fairburn sighed heavily once more. "Yes, indeed, our political system is a democracy, and as such, we must vote for a candidate who we feel will best represent our interests. That person, once elected, holds a seat in government, but as representative of an entire constituency, he or she can't always vote according to the wishes of an individual, however passionately he or she feels about an issue."

Dani frowned. "But, sir, almost all of the people don't want these townhouses."

"Yes, girls, and I support your cause, but once elected, a representative can't check with the people before voting or deciding on every issue. And I'm afraid that in this case your mayor ran on a campaign of fiscal responsibility and was elected by the majority of people to cut costs."

"So," Dani said, "politicians don't have to do what any of the people want once they get elected, even if the people no longer want the politician to do what got them elected so that the people have to wait until the next election."

Fairburn drummed his fingers impatiently on the doorframe. "Um, well, I wouldn't put it in quite such simplistic terms but, in fact, well ..." Then his shoulders sagged. "In a word, yes."

Dani snorted. "Well, I guess that answers that."

"We can't wait for the next election, right, Dani?" Caitlin said.

"Right."

"I'm sorry, girls, but compromise is the cornerstone of democracy, and I must say my afternoon has been rather compromised thus far. So if you'll excuse me."

Without another word the professor closed his door on the two frustrated girls, leaving them on the porch, puffing vapour into the chilly October afternoon air. For a few minutes Dani and Caitlin walked down the avenue in silence as windswept leaves cascaded around their reluctant retreat.

"Did you understand what the heck Professor Fairburn was talking about?" Caitlin finally asked.

"Not everything, but I've got another idea. Let's ask Sadie the same question about politics." And with a hop and skip she was already on her way to Abbotsford Home. "Come on, Caitlin, stop moping around. This is the time of day Sadie likes to play cribbage, and if we join her for a game or two, she'll tell us anything we want to know."

Caitlin's groan was lost in the wind and rattling leaves. "A game or two's fine. It's always losing loonies that's the trouble."

10
The Mystery of Winning at Cribbage

Sadie rubbed her hands in anticipation of playing cribbage and winning more loot. "Come on in, girls. Caitlin, you look frozen. And, Dani, you've got leaves in your hair."

"I am."

"I do?"

"Take a load off and tell these old bones the latest news before we start the game."

Dani scratched her head until Caitlin helped her untangle a mangled leaf from a coiled pigtail.

Sadie studied the girls' expressions down the length of her nose through the glasses perched on the end. "Why the long faces, girls? You know, if you stick with it, you'll beat me in cribbage yet. Besides, if you're short on loonies, I'll give you credit at Sadie's Credit Union."

"It's not that," Dani said, stroking her chin. "Caitlin and I are trying to think of a way to convince politicians not to put up townhouses in her park and on my family's old farm next to Gatineau Park, too. My dad's especially upset about the townhouses in the Gatineau."

"Politicians! Lunatics, all of 'em!" Sadie snapped.

"We even went to see Professor Dustin Fairburn, and he told us politicians can do whatever they want 'cause the people voted for them, so it doesn't matter what the people want."

"And we just can't let Windsor Park be sold for the *deficit*," Caitlin added. "Even if democracy is a compromise."

"Oh, so you got the brainy version from the old prof, did you?"

The girls nodded.

Sadie snorted. "The thing about politics is that people never tell it the way it is."

"What do you mean, Sadie?" Caitlin asked.

"Politicians think people are nincompoops who can't face the truth about life, so they sugarcoat, stretch, and finagle everything so no one really knows what the heck's goin' on."

"You mean sometimes politicians actually lie?"

Sadie smiled, and her teeth seemed to move in her mouth. "Politicians often talk in near-truths, half-lies, and broken promises, but unless a body hits the nail on the head every time, it amounts to a lie." She leaned forward. "And the public doesn't care enough to catch on."

"How do you know all that, Sadie?" Caitlin asked.

"'Cause we vote 'em right back in next election even if they've done nothin' but stretch the truth for years."

"So, Sadie," Dani said, "are you saying that if you're elected and you don't always tell the truth, you can get elected again?"

Sadie's eyes narrowed. "The game's called hypocrisy,

girls. That's when a body says one thing and does another. There's too many politicians using fancy words to hide the plain truth."

Dani's fist hit Sadie's table with a bang. "Oops, sorry, Sadie."

"No worry, girl. I like your thunder."

Dani shook her sore hand. "Well, we're going to have to find a way to make politicians tell the truth, right, Caitlin?"

Caitlin spat out the French braid she was chewing. "Sure, Dani, but how?"

"Ha," Sadie squawked, "the sixty-four-thousand-dollar question, for sure. But I gotta feelin' you're not tellin' me everything."

"Well …" Dani hesitated.

"Come on, out with it." Sadie waved a bony arm like a magic wand. "You know whatever it is, I won't ask for your source."

Dani exhaled. "Some people might get hurt if they're against the townhouses."

"And maybe worse has already happened," Caitlin said.

"Hmm, serious stuff." Sadie's watery blue eyes stared into space. "Tell you what. I'm gonna give you the home phone number of my grandnephew. He's a cop and a nice man, too. Tom Farrell's his name, and if you need some help, well, he's your man." With a shaky hand Sadie wrote down Officer Farrell's phone number on a slip of paper. "Now, girls, you have to promise me you'll call him so these old bones don't worry nights about you."

"Thanks, Sadie," Dani said, taking the piece of paper, "and we can start our game of cribbage now."

"Now promise me you'll call my grandnephew," Sadie insisted, peering at the girls with hawk-like eyes.

"We promise," Dani said.

"Yeah, we promise," Caitlin echoed with a mischievous grin, "to tell Officer Tom *everything*, 'cause he'll want to know how many loonies we've lost so far."

Sadie's intense eyes darted to Caitlin. "Well, *everything* might be a bit too much information. He's a busy man, so just concern yourselves with the facts in the case." Sadie adjusted her glasses and shifted uneasily in her chair.

Both girls grinned.

"You don't have to worry about us," Dani said. "Mum's the word."

Sadie glanced at one girl, then the other. A high-pitched laugh followed. "You had me goin' for a while, girls. Now let's start that game and maybe, just maybe, I'll take it easy this time." She winked. "Just in case I get in trouble with the law."

"We'll take our chances, Sadie," Dani said.

"'Cause we know," Caitlin said, "when we finally win a game of cribbage from you —"

"We'll have beaten the best," Dani finished.

The girls exchanged high-fives, and Sadie chuckled. "It's a painful truth, girls, but it is the truth."

"Hey, Sadie, maybe you should teach cribbage to all the politicians," Dani suggested.

"'Cause then they'd have to tell the truth," Caitlin added.

Sadie placed bony fingers on each girl's hand. "Don't have to, because I gotta feelin' you two will teach them the lesson of their lives."

"That's right," Dani said. "We'll teach them. Now let's play. I feel lucky."

"Like lambs to slaughter …" Sadie said under her breath.

11
Kids in the Sandbox

Caitlin and Dani waited at the police station information desk as people rushed back and forth, anxious to be on time for their important appointments. Dani checked her watch.

"What time is it?" Caitlin asked for the umpteenth time.

"It's 5:16. He's late."

"Maybe he doesn't have a watch like you to check every minute," Caitlin said.

Dani ignored her friend and glanced at her watch again. "Darn, it's 5:17."

"If you weren't my best friend, I'd clock you."

"I'm afraid if you did that I'd have to arrest you."

The girls jumped, turned quickly, and looked up at a big, grinning face attached to a policeman's navy blue uniform.

"Nancy Drew, I presume?"

"No, Officer," Dani said, "my name's Sherlock, and this is Watson."

The policeman laughed. "Great-Auntie was right. You two are a riot. My name's Tom Farrell. I'm sorry I'm a bit late. I had to deal with a … a customer who wasn't sure he wanted to stay at our, uh, hotel here tonight."

"We're real glad to meet you, Officer Tom," Caitlin said.

"I understand you girls have something I may be able to help you with."

Dani's eyes darted left and right down the corridor.

Officer Farrell's grin returned. "Oh, I see, top secret. Tell you what. Let me drive you home and you can explain your concern." He led the girls outside and down the stairs toward a police cruiser parked out front.

"Wow!" Dani said when she saw the cruiser.

"Cool!" Caitlin said.

Officer Farrell held the back door open and the girls clambered in.

"Dani, we're like prisoners," Caitlin whispered.

"Cool!" Dani said.

Officer Farrell pulled the car into the traffic. "So where to, girls?"

"Let's go to your house, Caitlin." Dani suggested.

"Okay. It's Belmont Avenue in Old Ottawa South."

"Gotcha. I know the neighbourhood. Now, girls, tell me what's up."

Dani stroked her chin as Caitlin chewed one of her French braids, both unsure what to say and how to start.

"Well …" Dani began.

"The thing is …" Caitlin tried.

"We sort of wondered …" Dani attempted again.

Tom looked at the girls in the rearview mirror. "Yes … come on …"

The girls were speechless for a few moments.

Tom's ever-present grin widened. "Let me guess. You'd like to report a schoolyard bully?"

Caitlin spit out her braid, and Dani folded her arms for dramatic effect.

Tom continued his teasing. "Or maybe you'd like to report a gambling ring in Abbotsford Home led by that shady ringleader, the artful and ageless Sadie Squires?"

"You know about that?" Caitlin blurted.

Dani tightened her arms around herself like a straitjacket. "As a matter of fact, we need you to investigate —"

"Murder!" Caitlin finished.

Tom's grin left his face for the first time, and his dark eyebrows knitted together. "Murder's a very serious charge, girls. It's not a good idea to report such serious matters unless there's real evidence."

"Actually, it's two murders," Caitlin corrected.

Dani loosened her death grip on herself. "Yeah, that's right, two murders."

Tom whistled. "Okay, girls, where are the two dead bodies?"

"Buried," Caitlin said simply.

"Buried?" Tom echoed.

"Yep, in their coffins," Dani said, "'cause no one else knows they were murdered."

Tom nodded. "Uh-huh, right. Does anyone even know they're dead?"

Dani placed her hands on the back of Tom's seat. "Of course. It's like this, Officer Tom. They were poisoned 'cause they were against the land developers in the parks."

"And one of the parks is Windsor Park near where I live," Caitlin added.

"Right," Dani said. "And the other park is Gatineau."

"Where Prime Minister Mackenzie King lives, except he's dead now," Caitlin said.

The girls noticed Tom's eyebrows rise. "Uh-huh, come to think of it, Sadie did say you two liked playing detective —"

"Especially Dani," Caitlin confirmed.

Dani pulled on her overall straps. "Well, I guess we do kind of like detective work, just like Sadie likes to play cribbage."

"So are you girls writing a detective novel? Maybe doing a little research, riding in a police cruiser —"

"He thinks we're kidding!" Caitlin whispered to Dani.

Dani huffed and puffed. "Kidding! Officer Tom, we'd never kid about real serious stuff like murder."

"Okay, so if these two people were actually murdered, how is it nobody knows?"

"Because everyone thinks they died naturally," Dani said.

"How can dying be natural?" Caitlin asked.

Tom turned the cruiser onto Bank Street. "And if everyone else thinks they died of natural causes, why do Great-Aunt Sadie's favourite twelve-year-olds feel otherwise?"

Dani wrinkled her nose as if the answer was obvious. "'Cause one was a city councillor and the other was some important guy with the National Capital Commission and both were against giving parks away to developers. And … and because … because …"

"Nice neighbourhood," Tom said, grinning as he steered the cruiser onto Belmont.

"Officer Tom," Dani said, eyes wide, "you don't believe us, do you?"

"Well, I'm kind of stuck on this matter of evidence."

A police dispatcher's voice suddenly cut into their conversation.

"Did that guy on the radio say something's happening at Windsor Park?" Caitlin asked.

Tom flicked a switch and picked up the radio mike. "This is Officer Farrell. Can you confirm a 10-11F at Windsor Park?"

"That's correct," the dispatcher said. "A 10-11F at Windsor Park."

"Roger. I'll respond. I'm in the vicinity. But maybe you should send some backup just in case."

"What's a 10-11F?" Dani asked, wrinkling her forehead.

"A fight," Tom said as he drove toward the park and pulled up to the curb near the entrance. Getting out of the cruiser, he was all business as he scanned the cluster of baby carriages and children ringing the kids' swings and monkey bars. In the distance, away from the play area, three figures were huddled. With Dani and Caitlin trailing him, Tom started off in that direction, then remembered who he had with him.

"Listen, girls, you better stay at the cruiser until my backup gets here. This could be dangerous."

The girls nodded, then continued to follow Officer Tom at a distance. As they got closer to the three arguing adults, they saw an old woman talking into a cell phone while two elderly gents circled each other threateningly.

"What are they doing?" Caitlin whispered to Dani loud enough for everyone to hear, including Officer Tom, who whirled around and scowled when he spotted the girls.

Before Tom could say anything, the old woman stared at the three newcomers and shouted, "They're fightin'. That's why I called the police. My old man's the short fat one. His name's Popeye Whittle. It sure as heck didn't take you long to get here."

"What seems to be the trouble?" Tom asked with authority.

"Trouble? Trouble?" the old man called Popeye yelled. "I'll tell you what the trouble is. This bloodsuckin' land grabber's the trouble, that's what."

"Old Man …" Dani started.

"Mitchell," Caitlin finished.

"I'm … I'm trouble?" Mitchell sputtered as he lunged at Popeye and missed with a right hook. "I'll tell you what the trouble is. This old kook thinks he can assault a law-abidin' citizen and businessman who has every legal right to walk on his own land. But he's messin' with the wrong fella 'cause I'll show him a thing or two about boxin'. I won a few bouts in my time."

Popeye weaved and bobbed like a prizefighter in slow motion. "You'll show me somethin' about boxin', will ya? Well, I'll box your ears till you listen to what I gotta say about low-life land filchers."

"Land filcher? Why, I'll —"

"Gentlemen!" Tom said.

The old men continued circling each other, ducking, shuffling their feet, and brandishing their fists menacingly.

"Gentlemen!" Tom shouted with even more force. Then, for good measure, he let loose with an ear-splitting whistle.

This time the old men stopped in their tracks and sagged against each other, completely out of breath.

"That's better," Tom said. "Now what seems to be the trouble on this fine October afternoon?"

Popeye squinted and pointed at Mitchell with his pipe, which he had taken out of his pocket and was trying to light. "This old coot don't even know what trouble is yet."

He's just like the cartoon Popeye the sailor, only chubbier, Dani thought.

Mitchell started rotating his fists again. "Land grabber,

eh? Try trespassin' on my land after I smack you proper, then you'll be both trespassin' and just plain ugly."

Popeye's face contorted, one eye closed, the other a narrow slit. He seemed to be pondering his strategy, then suddenly stuck out his substantial belly and rammed his opponent. Popeye's weight was too much for Mitchell's thin frame. The developer's fists fell to his side, his feet rocked, and his knees were about to give out when he grabbed Popeye's overalls. Both men swayed and twisted off balance, appeared to steady for a moment, then collapsed together onto a child's sandcastle. After several minutes of grunting and struggling to get up, both men gave up and lay back in the sand, exhausted.

"So, gentlemen, let's begin again, shall we?" Officer Tom suggested as he walked over to the two combatants and knelt on one knee beside them.

Popeye pushed himself onto an elbow, decided it was too much effort, and quit. Mitchell didn't even try to rise.

Guess they're going to let sleeping dogs lie, Dani thought.

Bet they could make cool sand angels lying there, Caitlin thought.

"Man's a crook!" Popeye finally gasped.

"Man's on my property!" Mitchell spat back.

"I see …" Tom frowned and pushed his hat to the back of his head. "Well, as you probably know at your ages, if you get up and start swinging again, I'll have to take you in."

Neither man moved, and Caitlin wondered if they were feeling cozy in the sand. *Maybe they'll take a nap together,* she thought.

Popeye coughed some sand out of his mouth. "I been livin' beside Windsor Park for fifty-three years, payin' my taxes, raised six kids, thirty-one grandchildren, four great-grandchildren so far, and then I find out this crook's gonna build fancy townhouses on my park. Well, I got news for him. It's never gonna happen."

Mitchell glared at his adversary. "I bought this land fair and square from the city, so don't tell me what I can't do. I've built houses right across this country, and I'm gonna build more here and across the river next to Gatineau Park whether you like it or not."

"Across the river next to Gatineau Park means on your family's old farm!" Caitlin cried.

"Thanks, Watson," Dani said. "Great deduction."

"You're welcome, Sherlock."

Tom rubbed his chin. "Well, now, let's see. I could easily arrest you both —"

"What for?" Popeye growled.

Tom leaned over and touched the short old man's belly. "Assault with a deadly weapon for one."

"And trespassin', too," Mitchell added.

"When I drove in here five minutes ago, this was still Windsor Park," Tom said. "As far as I know, the land transfer isn't complete yet. So I could arrest you both for public mischief."

"What?" both old men yelled.

Tom grinned. "Take a look under your backsides — both of you."

Popeye and Mitchell raised their heads and rested on their elbows. With obvious effort they rolled partially over on one cheek and inspected the lump under their backsides.

"Nothin' there," Mitchell mumbled.

"Just a bunch of sand," Popeye rasped.

"A bunch of sand that was a child's sandcastle before you guys vandalized his or her's creative piece of property."

Both men began to protest until Tom held up a finger and whistled again, which halted their griping. "So if you both would like to avoid being arrested today, here's what I want you to do. You'll both work together to build this heap of sand back into a castle."

"What the heck?" Popeye puffed.

"You can't make us do that," Mitchell cried, scattering leaves, sand, and dandruff from his scalp.

"That's true," Tom said calmly. "I can't make you do it. I can only guarantee that if you don't, I'll arrest both of you."

"That's blackmail!" Popeye bleated, squinting.

"What's blackmail?" Caitlin asked Dani.

"I think it's when your mail gets dirty from being dropped in the sand."

"Oh, right, makes sense … I guess. Dani, I'll be right back."

Maybe it makes sense, Dani thought, *but what in the world does blackmail really mean?*

Moments later Caitlin returned, out of breath. "Got it."

"What?"

Caitlin stepped forward and pointed to her camera. "I'll bet Double J would like a picture of this."

The two old men didn't look up as they struggled to recreate a skill not practised by them for over seventy years. Tom coached them patiently. "Pile it high in the middle. Now fill that bucket, pack it hard, and dump it over here."

"Ha, it works!" Mitchell cried out like a kid.

"We could do a circle of 'em around the castle," Popeye offered.

"You've done this before," Mitchell said to Tom.

"Oh, yeah. My three boys give me lots of practice. Now hollow out a trench around the whole thing. Kids love a moat to protect the castle."

"How about this twig for the flag at the top of the castle?" Popeye suggested.

Tom shrugged. "It's up to you and your partner."

Mitchell studied the structure, then said, "Why the heck not?"

Popeye proudly crowned the castle with his carefully chosen twig.

Tom rose from his haunches and cracked the knuckles on both hands. "Gentlemen, my work here is done." He led the girls back toward the cruiser, where another police car had just pulled up. Tom told the other officer the situation had been taken care of, then returned to the girls.

"That was good work, Officer Tom, keeping them from fighting and getting the sandcastle built again," Caitlin said.

"Like I said, I've had lots of practice," Tom said.

"You mean arresting criminals and bad guys?" Dani asked.

"No, I meant my three boys."

"Makes sense," Caitlin said.

Tom grinned. "Yeah, they're a handful, but they've taught me a lot."

"Is that because they know more than you do?" Caitlin asked innocently.

"Well, not exactly. It's just that kids have a way of doing, seeing things …"

"In a way adults have forgotten about," Dani finished.

"Yeah , that's it. Childhood wisdom, I suppose."

"So shouldn't you listen to what we're telling you about those two murders …" Dani started.

"'Cause we're kids, you know, and we definitely know something important," Caitlin finished.

Tom sighed. "I was afraid you'd start that up again."

"Well, murder's important, isn't it?" Dani asked.

"Of course it's important. But like I keep telling you, we need evidence."

Dani grabbed her overall straps as if she were about to give a speech on election day. "They were both poisoned, the city councillor and the important commission guy. They thought they were drinking something harmless a week ago, and if you dig them up, you could test to see if there's poison still in their bodies."

"And maybe tea, too," Caitlin added.

"An autopsy, you mean?" The grin disappeared from Tom's face. "I can't begin to tell you girls how difficult it would be for me to convince my commanding officer to do that, so please give me one good reason why I should try the impossible and risk my career without evidence."

"Okay," Dani said, "we'll give you one good reason."

"I'm listening."

"Sadie Squires."

"I'm afraid the only thing Great-Aunt Sadie knows about crime is that cribbage really does pay."

"Sadie kind of predicted you wouldn't believe us," Dani said.

"'Cause we're just kids," Caitlin added.

Tom was about to object, but Dani spoke first. "So she said to remind you when you were a kid and needed an adult to believe something."

"Something important," Caitlin added.

"And Great-Aunt Sadie was the only adult who'd listen to me, believe in me," Tom said, looking off into the distance and getting misty-eyed. He took a breath. "I don't know if I can do anything, but I'll think about it. That's all I can promise."

"Please try," Dani said.

"For Sadie's sake," Caitlin said.

Tom's grin returned. "That woman's probably taken about a million dollars from me in cribbage so far, but she's always been my favourite great-aunt."

"How many great-aunts do you have?" Caitlin asked.

"She's my favourite in a group of one."

"Officer Tom, did you say you and Sadie have gambled?" Dani asked.

"Guilty as charged."

"Well, if you don't want us to report you to the police, you have to believe us or else you and Sadie will have to …"

"Build a sandcastle," Caitlin finished.

Tom laughed as he got into the cruiser. "By the way, how much have you two lost to Sadie?"

"About a million," Caitlin replied.

"Ha! Now I believe you," Tom said, then drove away.

"Now what do we do?" Caitlin asked.

"Let's build a sandcastle and think about it," Dani answered.

"Sorry, Dani. We don't want people building houses in our park."

It was too late, though. Dani was already a stride ahead on her way to the sandbox.

12
Double Murder for Double J

Usually toward the end of October the fall colours were long past their peak in the Gatineau Hills. But September had been unusually warm, causing the colours of the fall foliage to remain vibrant. Driving along Highway 5 across the Ottawa River in Quebec and through Gatineau Park, Dani's dad, John, his two daughters, and their best friends couldn't help but notice the startling glow of red and yellow captured in the blinding noontime sunshine. As the van left the highway for River Road, the fall colours seemed even more brilliant framed against the cobalt-blue of the Gatineau River.

"I'm really glad you girls decided to come and see the beauty of the fall colours again," John said.

No one answered. Dani and Caitlin left Dani's dad in a state of blissful ignorance, since their motive was solving murder. Samantha and Kathleen left Dani's dad in a state of blissful ignorance, since their motive was the possibility of a teenage rendezvous. Dani and Caitlin further left Dani's dad in a state of truly blissful ignorance, since they hoped to learn something about the murder case from the teenage rendezvous.

John interpreted this conspiring silence as natural awe in the face of nature. As the van rounded a curve, they crossed railway tracks that were still used to take people on trips down memory lane on an old steam train. The steam train journey ended in the town of Wakefield, now in full view nestled along a wide section of the Gatineau River.

"Oh, look," John said, perched on the edge of his seat, "doesn't the covered bridge look absolutely beautiful? The original bridge stood for over a hundred years but was destroyed by arson about twenty years or so ago. The town rallied and rebuilt it just like the original. Of course, the Gatineau was an important river for the lumber industry, linking to the Ottawa River …"

As John rambled on, Caitlin asked Dani, "What's an arson?"

Her friend pondered the query for a moment, then said, "I think it's when parents have a son who does bad things like burn down bridges."

"So they won't be too happy to say he's *our son*?" Caitlin asked.

Dani grinned, a little relieved. "Yeah, that's it."

People eating ice cream and french fries glanced up as the van's brakes brought the vehicle to a screeching stop in front of the Wakefield General Store. The girls spotted Double J and Pipsqueak Pete among the happy munchers. Between four teenagers seeking a chance meeting, nothing was left to chance.

"Look who's there," Samantha said.

"What a coincidence!" Kathleen cried.

"What a coincidence!" Dani and Caitlin mimicked from the third row in the van.

"Who'd have thought … what are the chances?" John said, still in a peaceful state of blissful ignorance.

The teenage boys and girls moved slowly and painfully together like magnets in slow motion.

"So you really liked reading Charles Dickens?" Kathleen asked Double J.

The big, awkward boy nodded shyly.

Pipsqueak darted around both sides of his friend, ducking under Double J's right arm, then hopping high to gaze over the Goliath's left shoulder. "Double J read that book you gave him in no time flat. In fact, Old Man Mitchell kept yelling at Double J to quit reading and get back to work. He said life's not for playing in a sandbox and that Double J better get used to reality or else he'd amount to nothing at all."

Pipsqueak weaved and bobbed, dripping ice cream here and there as Caitlin searched in her knapsack. Ice cream splashed onto Nikki's willing snout. Delighted with his fortune, the dog immediately went cross-eyed and spent the next ten minutes trying to lick up the troublesome treasure.

"See?" Dani said proudly. "Most dogs can chase their own tails, but only Nikki can chase his own tongue!"

Grinning, Caitlin pulled out the photo of Old Man Mitchell and Popeye building a sandcastle in Windsor Park and showed it to Double J and Pipsqueak. Shock registered on both of their faces.

Did I hear Double J's jaw hitting the ground? Dani thought.

With a twinkle in her eye Caitlin said, "Maybe that fly in your mouth thinks your tonsils are an upside-down ice-cream cone."

"Where did you get that?" Kathleen asked, not knowing why the photo was so important but not liking being out of the loop one bit.

"Why would anyone care about two old men making a sandcastle?" Samantha asked dismissively.

With a trembling hand Double J slowly lifted the photo of his grandfather out of Caitlin's willing fingers. The older girls waited impatiently, not comprehending but knowing something was up. The younger girls waited patiently, wicked grins plastered on each of their mischievous faces. Slowly, a smile crept across Double J's big mug.

"He's never seen the old man taking time off from work and having fun," Pipsqueak informed them. "You have to admit it's really something. I mean, just look. The old guy's actually building a sandcastle and *smiling*."

"Yeah," Double J said in wonderment.

"But what does it all mean?" Kathleen fumed, unable to contain her frustration at not knowing something. Everyone stopped talking and waited for Double J to answer. But the big teenager took his time pondering the imponderable, the wry smile never leaving his face. Then slowly, carefully, he said, "It means Grandpa …"

"He calls him Grandpa. Double J calls Old Man Mitchell Grandpa," Pipsqueak piped up, clarifying the obvious.

Double J didn't seem to notice the interruption. "Grandpa was young once, and I guess he still remembers …"

"Remembers what?" Kathleen and Samantha both asked.

"How to play," Double J said simply.

"Oh," Kathleen and Samantha said, still not knowing what he was talking about.

"Oh," Dani and Caitlin said, knowing exactly what he meant.

"Oh," John said, just to be agreeable. Then he looked at the girls. "Well, how about we get some ice cream?"

"It's time for something healthy," Kathleen said, wrinkling her pert nose.

"I'd like a twelve-grain-and-soy muffin," Samantha said, moving toward the general store.

With the snooping sisters and dozy dad temporarily gone, Dani went straight into detective mode. "Double J, we noticed your grandpa likes to build things, and we kind of wondered how he was able to buy Windsor Park and my family's former farm next to Gatineau Park?"

"Yeah," Caitlin said, no longer smiling, "'cause parks aren't supposed to be for sale and Dani's family farm should be part of Rex's park."

A mystified expression crossed Double J's face. "Who?"

"Uh, forget what Caitlin said," Dani said in her best detective voice. "Just answer the question."

Double J frowned. "Believe me, I wish Grandpa didn't want to build his townhouses where's he doing it."

"Old Man Mitchell says people are better off watching TV in their own townhouses than wasting time in a park," Pipsqueak volunteered.

"But how did he know how to buy the land if it wasn't for sale?" Dani asked.

Double J's eyebrows dropped and angled, making him look like a big sad puppy. "Grandpa, Grandpa …"

"Double J's trying to say that Old Man Mitchell fixed the City Council and the NCC. Fixed it, like in the movies." Pipsqueak always moved a little faster when delivering important information. Now he was bouncing around as if someone had lit a fire under him.

"Is that true Double J?" Dani pressed. "Did your grandpa

do something illegal?"

Double J bit his lip and nodded. "I heard him talking on the phone to Jerry Skinner, who works for Grandpa, about making sure nobody finds out. Ever!"

Caitlin swallowed and fired off the inevitable question. "Find out what?"

Double J sighed. "That's why I like that picture of Grandpa building the sandcastle. I figure if he could've just played sometimes, he wouldn't have had to do what he did."

As soon as Dani picked her jaw off the sidewalk, she asked, "What did he do?"

"He told Jerry to fix it with the City Council and the NCC so they'd vote to sell the land for his townhouses."

"They must've done something, too, 'cause next thing you know Old Man Mitchell's got the land," Pipsqueak said.

Double J's chest heaved. "I'm not very proud of the work we're doing."

"Are the children boring you two with talk of beagle tricks and kindergarten adventures?" Kathleen asked as she returned from the general store.

"Don't worry," Samantha said. "We're here to rescue you from further tales from the sandbox."

Caitlin and Dani eased away from the group as Nikki wrapped himself around his master's legs. As discussion moved back to Charles Dickens, Dani whispered to her friend, "Caitlin, Old Man Mitchell must be the murderer."

"Poor Double J," Caitlin said. "All he wants to do is read and have some fun once in a while. *Omigosh!* If Old Man Mitchell's the murderer, and Double J's working for his grandpa, maybe they'll think he's guilty, too. What do we do, Dani?"

Dani's serious expression never changed as she untangled herself from her ice-cream-eating hound.

"Caitlin, there's only one thing we can do. We have to solve these murders, even if Old Man Mitchell and Double J go to prison!"

As Nikki discovered a tasty piece of barely chewed gum on the sidewalk, Caitlin's question captured the bleakness of the moment. "Guess they don't build sandcastles in prison, do they?"

13
Something to Prove

The girls had a lot of important things on their minds and decided to have a sleepover at Caitlin's house on Sunday night, particularly since Monday was a professional development day for teachers and they didn't have school. Somehow, desperately, they felt that if they were near the park they could protect it. Up in Caitlin's attic, overlooking the park, the girls discussed vital business like murder and Halloween costumes without prying adult and adult wannabes getting in the way. Nikki was more interested in the sounds of the wind and the rain than in what the girls were saying. His ears twitched with every gust of wind and crash of thunder. The girls lay on their backs on Caitlin's bed gazing up at the streaks of lightning through the skylight. The girls had been ready for bed for a long time but were nowhere near ready for sleep. Besides, what fun would a sleepover be if all you did was sleep?

"I just can't imagine Windsor Park full of townhouses," Caitlin said morosely.

"And Dad looks like he's going to pee his pants whenever he thinks about Mitchell's townhouses on the old O'Neill Farm," Dani said.

Nikki moved from his position between the girls and began circling in search of the perfect snooze position. After a couple of hundred rotations, either he had found perfection or else was too dizzy to go on, so he thumped down. Once settled, Nikki snorted air from his snout until, like a balloon, it lay lifeless and airless. Sleep was instantaneous.

"See, Nikki's upset, too," Dani said, "so he's gone to sleep."

"I bet he sleeps twenty-two hours a day already."

"I know what he usually does, but lately he's been sleeping about an hour longer, poor little guy."

"I wonder how long he'd sleep if someone stole his food?"

"I just know Officer Tom's gonna come through for us," Dani said, ignoring Caitlin's question. "They have to listen to a policeman who thinks there's a murder, right?"

A cloud hung over the murder case, not to mention over Caitlin's house. Sheets of rain pounded the skylight, and the girls pulled the covers up to their chins defensively. After the longest time, Caitlin finally asked, "What are you wearing on Halloween?"

"Dunno yet. It depends. If Officer Tom can convince people to do an autopsy on the murdered victims, I think I'll go as a policewoman. You?"

"I'm going as a go-go dancer. My Aunt Donna says I can use her stuff from the 1960s, only I think I'm going to dye her red wig blue. What do you think, Dani?"

Only the busy drone of the pelting rain answered Caitlin.

"Dani, it'll soon be Halloween. What are we going to do if Officer Tom can't come through?"

A flash of lightning filled the skylight, and a boom of

thunder immediately followed. Nikki's ears twitched from the commotion, but it didn't coax him out of his blissful slumber in beagle heaven. Dani finally remembered to breathe and exhaled about fifteen litres of air. Then she answered Caitlin's question. "Don't know, but I'm thinking of a plan."

"A plan? To do what?"

"Something to help solve the murders and convince politicians not to sell parks to build houses."

"Oh, is that all?" Caitlin said.

Another clap of thunder seemed to seal the mood of hopelessness and doom. The girls continued to lie awake on their sleepover for the longest time. Only Nikki, the ever-sensitive canine, treated the sleepover for what it was and slept selfishly all night long.

At exactly seven the next morning the doorbell rang. Up on the third floor the girls were finally sleeping soundly. Nikki, too, slept like the dead, happy to snooze, as always, whenever possible. Caitlin's dad, Bob, had just woken up and was preparing for his morning run. Dani's dad was on his way over to run with his friend. The unexpected ring of the doorbell allowed Bob to abandon his sad attempt at stretching. As he lumbered over to the door on his pair of unstretched two-by-fours, he was both surprised to hear the bell and a bit relieved that he no longer had to try to stretch. "Not like John to be so early," he muttered.

When Bob opened the front door and saw Officer Tom Farrell standing there, he was unable to suppress a large gulp but relaxed somewhat at Tom's easy smile. "Good morning, and it's a nice bright one after that monsoon last night. I was just wondering if Caitlin and Dani might both be here and if I might have a word with them."

A couple of dozen questions coursed through Bob's mind before he finally said, "Um, yeah, sure. I'll get them."

The girls stumbled down the stairs, wiping sleep from their eyes. Nikki soon followed, howling with indignation at having his beauty sleep cut so short.

Bob pointed upstairs to the bathroom and mumbled, "Be right back."

Tom seemed amused by the situation he had caused even as he apologized for it. "Sorry, girls, I guess I didn't figure on seasoned detectives ever sleeping."

"That's okay, Officer Tom," Dani said. "We don't mind you waking us for important police business."

"'Cause we know it must be real important for you to come early like this," Caitlin said.

Tom's grin disappeared. "Well, actually, I'm afraid I came here to tell you that I tried to create some interest in your story but didn't have any luck."

Dani was suddenly wide awake. "But … but it's not a story. There really were two murders."

"Really!" Caitlin cried.

"Well, whatever really happened," Tom said, "it didn't happen according to the law unless there's evidence."

As Dani struggled to find words of protest, Nikki's howl registered objection loud and clear.

"I'm really sorry, girls. I wish I could do more." Tom slid his cap toward the back of his head. "Truth is, the captain thought I was plain nuts for even bringing up the whole idea of an autopsy without real evidence."

"Isn't there anything you can do?" Dani pleaded.

"Sure. Just as soon as you get some real evidence for me. That is, if I want to keep my job."

"If you lose your job, you can always build sandcastles in

the park with your sons," Caitlin suggested.

Tom sighed. "Ha. There are some days I'd like nothing better."

"But this is a real murder case," Dani said, folding her arms tightly around herself to emphasize her point.

She could shake hands with herself behind her back if she wanted to, Caitlin thought. This notion amused Caitlin so much that she couldn't suppress a wicked little grin.

When Dani spotted Caitlin's smirk, she squeezed herself all the more. "This is no laughing matter, Caitlin, and besides, we have work to do, a murder to solve, parks to save ..."

Oh-oh, the poor girl's starting to sound like our older and wiser sisters, Caitlin thought, finally getting control of her facial expression.

Dani was worked up now and didn't even notice that her protests and declarations were drawing a crowd. Bob had clumped back down the stairs, and Samantha stood on the landing, listening but not amused. John arrived at the front door ready for his morning run with Bob. Kathleen trailed her father, ready to get a head start on her math homework with Samantha. People shifted uneasily until John asked the question that was on everyone's mind: "What the heck's going on?"

Tom Farrell glanced at the girls and saw their pleading expressions. Dani's bulging eyes made her seem particularly desperate. "Everything's fine, folks. These two observant young detectives witnessed an incident in the park the other day and I'm just following up. Nothing serious." He winked at the girls, and they both exhaled.

Dani grabbed her overall straps and rocked on the balls of her feet. *Officer Tom called us detectives,* she thought, *and he didn't tip off the others about our murder investigation.*

Well, we'll show him what evidence is. "Thanks, Officer Tom," she finally said.

"Dani!" John said, taking in the policeman's name tag. "You should be calling him Officer Farrell."

"That's okay, sir," Tom said, smiling. "I like being called Tom."

"'Cause that's his name," Caitlin said, wondering if her pesky sister, Samantha, had finished the last of the waffles.

Dani winked with obvious exaggeration. "Don't worry, Officer Tom. We'll get you that evidence."

"Evidence?" both fathers and the older sisters asked simultaneously.

"Yeah," Caitlin said, thinking there might be English muffins if the waffles were gone. "We have to prove that two old men knocked down a kid's sandcastle."

Panic crossed Tom's face. "Um …"

The eyes of all the adults and the two teenagers zeroed in on Caitlin.

"We could take turns spying from a tree to see if they return to the scene of the crime," Caitlin said, getting carried away. "Of course, most of the leaves are falling off the trees, so we'd better get the evidence before the end of November. But who'd want to sit in a tree for a month, anyway?"

Only the sound of Nikki's collar rattling from incessant scratching broke the silence that followed.

Finally, Bob managed a weak offer. "Can I get you a coffee, Officer Farrell?"

"No thanks, sir. I have to be going. And believe me, girls, you've done enough and no one's expecting you to find evidence. But thank you for your efforts and concern."

A glint of determination entered Dani's eyes. "Caitlin and I promise we'll get you the evidence you need to solve this crime. Right, Caitlin?"

"Right …" Caitlin said, her mind completely on food now and almost convinced there might be waffles still in the freezer.

Tom tipped his hat and was gone, the crowd quickly dispersed, and only Dani, Caitlin, and a scratching canine were left in the hallway. Caitlin decided waffles could wait and grabbed Dani by her overall straps. "How are we going to get evidence about two murders? And you promised!"

"That's 'cause I think we work best under pressure," Dani said, bounding up the stairs. "Come on, Caitlin, it's time we paid a friend of Mr. King's a visit."

"Huh?"

"Sure. Remember how Rex said that hanging around Bert Harper's statue on Parliament Hill would give us inspiration? And while we're getting there I can plan my Halloween costume."

Dani disappeared as Nikki rose to his feet and gave a ferocious shake, beginning with his head and ending with his rear end. Satisfied, he scrambled up the stairs after his master.

If that girl gets any nuttier, Caitlin thought, *she'll have to dress in a Halloween costume year-round.*

14
Strength in Numbers

Two hours and four waffles later the girls stepped off the bus at the corner of Bank Street and the Sparks Street Mall. The statue of Bert Harper was two blocks away in the shadow of the Peace Tower on Parliament Hill. The bright sunshine was particularly welcome after the storm of the night before. A strong northern wind created ripples in the leaf-choked puddles dotting the street. Dani bounced over one puddle and then dragged her running shoes through another as she became absorbed in the details of the case. Caitlin stepped around every puddle as she became engrossed in the elements of her next waffle breakfast.

"Mr. King thinks he actually saw the NCC guy being poisoned with a cup of tea," Dani said, "so he must know something we can use as evidence, only he doesn't know it 'cause he's not a detective like us."

I'll bet applesauce would be good with waffles, Caitlin thought. Then she said, mostly to herself, "Why would he know anything? He was only the prime minister of Canada."

"Exactly," Dani said, successfully leaping over an enormous puddle and landing in another smaller one. "Excellent!"

"Yuck!" Caitlin cried, spying the mud on her friend's shoes and overalls. "You know, Dani, it is possible to just walk around the puddles."

"And what fun would that be?"

As the girls crossed Wellington Street, Dani pulled out her map and compass. "Should be just east of here."

"Oh, east," Caitlin said absentmindedly, "and I thought you just turned right."

Dani stopped suddenly, and Caitlin ploughed into her with a grunt. *Now she decides to step around puddles,* Caitlin thought.

"There he is!" Dani declared.

"Who?"

"Bert Harper. Well, I mean his statue. And look, he's so important there's a crowd gathered around him. Mr. King was right about ol' Bert."

"Dani, that's not a crowd. It's only three people."

"Exactly. A crowd."

When the girls arrived at the statue, the three people who stood in front of it turned and registered disapproval. As it became clear that the girls weren't moving on, a tiny white-haired woman asked, "Can we help you?"

"Oh, no, thank you," Dani said. "We're just looking at ol' Bert here."

"Well, could you come back later?" the tallest, heaviest-set member of the trio suggested. "We're holding a meeting just now." He adjusted his beige scarf and flattened it against his beige shirt. Then he pulled a pen from behind his ear and a notepad from his beige shorts. "I'll take the minutes of the fifteenth convening of the WLMK Society."

"Sure is cold for shorts, mister," Dani said, who wore long-legged denim overalls year-round.

"Say, mister, are you an adult Boy Scout or do you just like dressing like one?" Caitlin asked. "Dani and I once disguised ourselves as Girl Guides, only that was in the summer and … oh, I get it, you're dressed for Halloween early."

The Boy Scout curled his lip and stood ramrod straight. "Certainly not."

"Mister!" Dani shouted at the third member of the group. "Your beard moved. Look, it's doing it again!"

The bearded man laughed and pulled a ferret from his collar. "His name's Ernie, and he just woke up. I think he wants to visit. Yes, he does. Come on, you can pet him. Watch this. I'll spray this on your arm and he'll love you forever."

Caitlin sniffed. "What's that stuff?"

"It's his special treat when he's a good boy, and he's such a good boy, aren't you?" the bearded man said, pursing his lips and pretending he was going to kiss his furry friend. The man and his ferret gazed at each other close up and touched whiskers.

They say pet owners start to look like their pets after a while, Caitlin thought. *I wonder what this guy used to look like.*

The Boy Scout wasn't amused. He harrumphed and wrote ferociously in his notebook. Satisfied with the speech he'd prepared, the Boy Scout opened his mouth to speak just as the tiny white-haired woman snapped, "Time to come to order, folks."

"I've prepared some introductory remarks on the importance of listening to the advice of elders, particularly well-read adults such as the members of our little society," the Boy Scout said.

"Well, save your breath for now," the white-haired woman insisted. "Since I'm president and you're vice-president, it's up to me to start this meeting."

The Boy Scout pouted. "I'm only vice-president because there were no other members to vote."

"Which makes me president of the WLMK Society this year. Next year you can be president and I'll be vice-president." The tiny woman said this with authority in spite of the fact that the top of her head didn't quite come up to the bottom of the Boy Scout's beige scarf.

"But what about these two?" the Boy Scout asked, as if Dani and Caitlin couldn't hear.

The white-haired woman adjusted her spectacles. "If these two young ladies would like to listen to the business of the WLMK Society, I don't see any harm. And maybe they'll want to be the first two people to sign our petition."

"For what?" Dani asked.

"What does WLMK stand for?" Caitlin asked.

The bearded man wrapped his ferret into a pretzel around his neck. "It stands for William Lyon Mackenzie King. We're members of his fan club."

"I keep telling you we're the executive members of a society, not a fan club," the Boy Scout said with annoyance.

"How about that," Dani said. "Rex isn't as forgotten as he thinks he is. He even has his own fan club."

The Boy Scout rolled his eyes.

"How many other members are there in Canada?" Dani asked. "Or is it even possible to count that high?"

"We're the executive members, founding members, and the only members of the WLMK Society," the white-haired woman said.

Dani picked at a leaf stem clinging to her messy pigtail.

"I don't understand."

"We only have three fans so far," the bearded man said, "but we're going to change all that. Maybe you two would like to join and then we'd be five."

"According to our Constitution, members must be at least sixteen years old," the Boy Scout growled.

"How old's your ferret?" Caitlin asked.

"That's right!" the bearded man cried. "Ernie could be a member, couldn't you, pal? In ferret years you're almost fifty."

"That's absurd!" the Boy Scout shouted, stamping his foot on the sidewalk.

"Order, order!" the white-haired woman piped up. "Enough chitchat. We have important agenda items to discuss and none more important than lobbying the federal government to commission a new statue to the late great Prime Minister William Lyon Mackenzie King next to this one of his dear friend and fellow musketeer, Bert Harper."

"Hear, hear," the Boy Scout said.

"Okay, we'll sign the petition," Dani said, "since we just happen to share your opinion of Canada's longest-serving prime minister." She pulled on her overall straps and rocked on the balls of her feet.

"My goodness," the white-haired woman said, "you know about our neglected leader!"

"Oh, sure," Dani said nonchalantly, examining her dirty fingernails. "We know all about Rex …"

"And his dog, Pat," Caitlin finished.

"See?" the bearded man said. "They understand how King's pet and loyal companion made a significant contribution to Canada's history."

"This is ridiculous!" the Boy Scout yelled, turning heads

along Wellington Street. "They can't sign the petition until they're sixteen."

The white-haired woman nodded. "I'm afraid that's true. It's in our Constitution. You have to be sixteen."

"Darn!" the bearded man said. "It's unfair to keep kids and pets out of Mackenzie King's fan club. How about if I make a motion to amend the Constitution?"

The Boy Scout turned red, then pulled an official-looking document out of his coat. "No, no, no! Our Constitution can only be changed with a two-thirds majority."

"You have a point," the white-haired woman said thoughtfully. "Of course, if I was to support a motion to amend our Constitution, there'd be a two-thirds majority and we'd be acting according to our Constitution as we vote to do away with it."

The Boy Scout scowled, then the three founding and only members of the WLMK Society engaged in a lively debate. Dani tried to speak to the group but was ignored. She attempted to get the group's attention by holding up her hands but was ignored. Finally, she put two fingers in her mouth and whistled louder than the Peace Tower clock chimes.

Heads turned up and down Wellington Street. More important, the fiercely debating white-haired woman, the bearded ferret man, and the annoyed Boy Scout all looked at the girls.

"The way I see it, we have two choices," Dani said, smashing her fist into the palm of her hand. *"Ouch!"* She glanced at her smarting hand for a moment before continuing. "Either you argue over changing all your rules, which won't help get a proper statue like this cool one for ol' Rex, or you let us try to help get the job done without joining your fan club."

The Boy Scout opened his mouth to speak but decided to smooth out his uniform instead.

"Yeah, 'cause we don't want to join or vote, but it would be kind of cool for a ferret to join," Caitlin said.

The bearded man and the Boy Scout were about to launch into another squabble, but the white-haired lady cut them off. "How in the world can you help, girls?"

"Yeah, Dani, what exactly is our plan?" Caitlin asked.

"Yes, well …"

She's waffling, Caitlin thought, remembering her breakfast.

"We, that is, me and Caitlin —"

"That would be Caitlin and I," the Boy Scout corrected.

"Yes, well, Caitlin and I have a plan to get a statue of Mackenzie King right over there, looking down at old Bert here."

The white-haired lady furrowed her already heavily wrinkled brow. "Yes, dear, but the question remains how?"

"Well, the thing is, I mean our plan … we can't tell," Caitlin stammered, "we're not allowed to tell 'cause we have a Kids' Constitution for *our* club."

"Yeah, that's right," Dani said, rising once more on the balls of her feet.

The Boy Scout snorted. "That's ridiculous!"

"We'd appreciate any help," the bearded man said, stuffing the ferret back into his shirt.

"We really should begin our meeting," the white-haired woman said.

The girls slowly backed away from the important conference in progress. They gazed for a moment at the statue of Bert Harper, Mackenzie King's best friend, forever a doer of deeds, a man of action, a hero.

"Guess we don't have a plan, do we, Dani?"

"No, but has that ever stopped us before?"

Caitlin knew better than to answer as she pondered what they were up against: one long-deceased prime minister and his equally dead dog, two unsolved murders that no one believed were murders, no clues, and one nutty fan club trying to convince Canadians to erect another statue of Mackenzie King on Parliament Hill.

"Dani, we don't need a plan. We need a miracle!"

"You're right, Caitlin. So let's go find one."

15
The Mystery of the Two-Headed Dog

"And so you see, Caitlin, not only do we have a plan, we have Plan B if Plan A doesn't work out," Dani said, skipping down the path toward Kingswood Cottage and the nearby lake. The girls had talked Dani's dad into taking them back up to the Gatineau, which hadn't been hard since he wanted to look at more cottages.

"But, Dani, Plan B is just repeating Plan A if it doesn't work," Caitlin said, always two strides behind her friend.

"Clever, isn't it?"

"Oh, boy!"

"You see," Dani said, attempting to prevent Nikki from charging at a squirrel, "people don't realize that a lot of detective work is to just keep trying — calm down, Nikki!"

Suddenly, Nikki stopped and stood perfectly still, a most uncharacteristic beagle trait. Only his ears moved, twitching rhythmically. Then his nose started searching for the scent. But even Nikki's hyper-sniffing ability couldn't discover the source.

Then, out of thin air, Pat's snout appeared next to Nikki's ultra-sensitive sniffer. "See, Caitlin, Nikki's just like a detective. Even though he can't see Pat, he knows something's there."

"Except that it's no mystery that Nikki's searching for food."

"No, Caitlin, look at him. I think he knows there's a ghost dog in front of him."

"Uh-huh, and I suppose he knows the ghost dog's a terrier named Pat who used to be the prime minister's pet."

"I think you're right, Caitlin, except I'm not sure he knows what colour Pat is. Dogs are colour blind, you know."

Caitlin opened her mouth to answer but decided there was no possible retort to Dani's opinions about dogs.

"Hey, here comes Mr. King," Dani said. "Hi, Rex!"

Out from a swirl of leaves and through a shaft of early-morning sunshine emerged the form of William Lyon Mackenzie King. "So glad to see you again, girls. I wasn't at all certain you were coming back. And who could blame you? It's asking a lot of you to act in a decisive manner at the tender age of twelve. And who am I to ask such a thing? After all, when I was prime minister and a lot older than you are, I almost always vacillated, obfuscated, and waffled when faced with a decision."

Waffled? Caitlin thought. *He must be talking about breakfast.*

"So if you're here to tell me you can't proceed I, more than anyone, will understand. Don't worry. Leave that to me, since worrying is my specialty. It's why I couldn't easily make decisions or live with those I made."

Before Caitlin could say, "Thanks for telling us. We're off the hook," Dani horned in with, "Well, Rex, you can stop fretting, because we're on the case, in *case* you didn't know."

"Excellent," King said, waving his walking stick.

"Only problem is, we need evidence and we think you can help."

King blinked. "Me? I've told you all I know. How can I possibly help?"

More of that waffling, Caitlin thought.

The long-dead prime minister shrugged. "Evidence is of the physical world and I am, most decidedly, of the spiritual world. The truth is all I know, not how to prove it."

"We know, Rex," Dani said, "but we can't get the police to believe us unless we can give them some hard evidence."

"You've actually talked to the police?"

"We sure have," Dani said.

"Well, I'm truly impressed. You've acted decisively and no doubt with determination."

"The big problem is the police don't believe us!" Caitlin said. "Kind of like Dani's dad when we said we wanted to come back here to study the history of Kingsmere."

"And now my dad wants evidence, too, like interesting facts and stuff about this place," Dani said.

"Now that kind of evidence I can help you with," King said. "But as for the other evidence ..."

"Maybe we can review the case at the scene of the crime," Dani said, hooking her thumbs under her overall straps.

Oh, boy, here she goes, Caitlin thought as the trio strolled along the path to the lake.

"Rex, when you saw that Williams guy poisoned here, you say he drank from a cup, right?"

"Yes, an actual teacup, fine china, in fact, but I only saw

the back of the person with Williams. I never got a good look at the murderer. In fact, as I told you earlier, I didn't know for sure it was murder until I read that the unfortunate Mr. Williams died that very night while driving his car — no doubt returning from the very same appointment with his killer."

"Right," Dani said, placing one foot on a log. "And what happened to that teacup?"

"The dastardly murderer must have taken it."

"Right," Dani said, resting her elbows on her knees and her chin on her hands. "Now, Rex, was there anything else left at the scene of the crime? Anything at all? Think carefully."

"Yes, yes. I appreciate the need for vigilance to detail," King said, becoming flustered, "but I simply can't think of anything that was left at the scene of the crime. Someone who had the presence of mind to collect the poison cup isn't likely to leave anything else."

"Right," Dani said, biting her lip with disappointment.

"But I do object to those who litter."

"Right," Dani repeated.

"What did you just say, Rex?" Caitlin asked.

"Litterers. Those who litter on these grounds, once mine but now belonging to the Dominion of Canada, are thoroughly objectionable."

"Right," Dani said, now suffering from a case of detective angst.

"Like who, Rex?" Caitlin prodded.

"Well, the murderer for one," King answered.

"Right," Dani said, thinking of other angles, plans, detecting strategies.

Caitlin frowned. "Dani, did you hear what Rex just said?"

"Huh? Of course, I heard and I promise never to throw a candy wrapper on the ground." Dani was about to replant her face on the palm of her hand when a thought occurred to her. "*Omigosh*, did you say *murderer*, Rex?"

"Yes, indeed. Although I never saw his or her face, I certainly noticed the culprit was littering while making a quick exit. In fact, I was particularly alarmed by the miscreant's discarded lit cigarette thrown into the forest."

"Did you go and find the cigarette?" Dani asked.

"And what else did the person throw away?" Caitlin asked.

"Of course, I retrieved the errant cigarette! It could have started a forest fire. And I also picked up an empty book of matches."

Dani took a deep breath. "Now, Rex, think carefully, 'cause this is very important. Where did you put those things?"

"I threw them into the trash, naturally."

"Where?" two voices asked as one.

"In the work shed where I leave all refuse from careless visitors. It's beside Moorside Cottage where the tearoom is, but it would have been taken away by now. How in the world, though, can this be relevant?"

"Can you take us there?" Dani asked.

"Yes, of course, though for what purpose I can't imagine. Oh, what am I saying? It's not as if I have other engagements. Come on, Pat, let's show your friend Nikki a place where he'll be most pleased."

As the strange group started up the path toward Moorside, Caitlin whispered, "You know, Rex, you almost made a joke about Nikki's eating habits."

"I was trying to do just that, actually," King whispered.

"Jolly good, Rex, and if you just added something about beagle fine dining on garbage, you'd have pulled it off," Caitlin suggested.

"Duly noted," King said.

When they arrived at the garbage shed, an odd thing happened. Just as Dani said, "Darn, it's locked," King and Pat stepped through the wooden planks and disappeared into the shed. A moment later the girls and Nikki heard the rattle of a latch, and the door opened from the inside.

"Cool!" Caitlin said.

"Wow!" Dani said. "See, Rex, you did that and you didn't even hesitate."

"I didn't, did I? Perhaps it is possible to learn something in my old ... er ... deceased age."

"And I thought you couldn't teach a dead dog new tricks," Caitlin said.

"Oh, yes, in our more than fifty years together as spirits I've been able to teach Pat quite a number of tricks."

"Kidding, Rex, just kidding," Caitlin said.

"Ah," King murmured, still not quite getting it.

Dani stepped across the threshold of the shed with earnest intent. "And where did you throw the evidence, Rex?"

King winced at the word *evidence*. "In this bin, regrettably long since emptied."

Dani sighed heavily. "Too bad."

Nikki blew out a deep breath, too, unhappy that a leash separated him from the object of his desire.

Caitlin also exhaled mightily, thinking of gelato and other good things. "I'm hungry."

Finally, King added his sigh to the symphony of released air. "Such a shame. Even in here litter is discarded outside the garbage bins." He reached down and distractedly picked up a few scattered items as the girls fumed over lost evidence and growing appetites. "Though I can't imagine it's possible, the emblem on this looks familiar. But how can that be? No, certainly not. But a fact is hard to ignore. Oh, dear, I feel as if I'm prime minister again."

"Come on, Rex, spit it out," Dani said. "How important can that be?"

"Yes, I'm almost certain. The crest is distinctive. It's a family's coat of arms!"

"Wow, and I thought it was just a Coke can," Caitlin said.

"Not the can," King said, his voice rising. "This matchbook. It's the very one dropped by the murderer."

"It must have fallen out of the garbage container when it was emptied," Caitlin said excitedly.

"This is important evidence for our case," Dani said, glancing around the shed as if more clues might be spotted.

"But what the heck does it prove?" Caitlin asked.

"Well," Dani started slowly, "it proves the murderer liked to smoke."

"Or light birthday candles," Caitlin added with a touch of sarcasm.

"May I make a suggestion?" King interjected. "I have a book in my study at Moorside that identifies family names with coats of arm such as we have here."

"Good thinking, Rex," Dani said, already striding toward Moorside. "Let's go!" When she reached the cottage's front door, she rattled it, then glowered. "Locked!"

King and Pat strolled toward the front door as if they were facing an open field. Just as they were about to pass through the locked door, King tipped his walking stick to his head and nodded at the girls.

"That's so cool," Caitlin said. "I wish I could do that." Then she shouted through the door, "Hey, Rex, can you and Pat do that backwards?"

"Caitlin, we don't have time to fool around," Dani said. "We have a case to solve, remember? Hey, where's Rex? I thought he was going to unlock the door."

Seconds later, as Dani fretted and Caitlin thought about food, King and Pat walked backwards through the front door of Moorside.

Caitlin laughed. "Rex, you look like Michael Jackson doing the moonwalk."

"Who?"

"Oh, I'm sorry," Caitlin said. "I guess he was before your time."

Dani rolled her eyes. "He was before *our* time, Caitlin. Is that the book, Rex?"

"Yes, indeed," King answered, sitting on a veranda step with the girls on either side.

"There must be hundreds of crests in there," Dani said.

"Thousands, in fact," King said.

Caitlin groaned, trying to calculate how long it would be before they could eat. After fifteen minutes of searching for the coat of arms in the enormous book, she asked shakily, "Anyone hungry?"

"No, I had a big breakfast," King said, "but thanks for reminding me that I'd better feed Pat."

"Huh?" Caitlin said, confused. "Ghosts can't eat …" Then she grinned. "Hey, not a bad joke, Rex!"

"I'm still learning, but perhaps that demonstrates some improvement."

"And look," Caitlin said, "I think Pat's trying to joke with Nikki."

The terrier put his snout close to Nikki as if attempting to lick the beagle, but instead he walked through Nikki until he stood with his head coming out of Nikki's rear end.

"Oh, my gosh, Dani, look, the two-headed dog!"

But Dani was more interested in what was in the book. "I found it! This is it for sure. And you won't believe it. The family name that goes with this coat of arms is ... Mitchell!"

16
Hounding Lucy

"Dani, you're as crazy as Nikki gets when he sees an old pizza crust," Caitlin said as Dani tried to hold Nikki back from eating pizza crust off an Ottawa sidewalk.

As soon as they had returned from their latest trip to Kingsmere, the girls had set off in search of Old Man Mitchell's place of business before it closed for day. Now, once again, Caitlin was trying to keep up with her friend's breakneck speed. "How the heck are we going to get evidence about a murder?"

"Two murders," Dani said breathlessly.

"Oh, right, two murders. That makes it much easier. But, Sherlock, can you please remind me how we're going to get evidence about two murders from the place where the murderer works?"

"Well, Watson, I'm not exactly sure. I just know that if we don't try, then two murders will never be solved for certain."

"But what do we say when we get there?"

"We'll think of something."

"I was afraid you'd say that," Caitlin said, but Dani was already two strides ahead, searching for a certain number on a building. She was looking for the Mitchell Development Company on Somerset Street, Nikki was hunting for more pizza crust, and Caitlin was trying to think of a reason not to look for anything except maybe for some gelato.

"There it is!" Dani finally cried.

Caitlin rolled her eyes. "Oh, joy!" Then she thought, *It's amazing what makes that girl happy.*

The girls stood in front of a three-storey brick Victorian mansion located between two trendy renovated restaurants. The house had once been among the most beautiful on the street but was becoming decrepit after many years of neglect.

Sure is suspicious for a guy who wants to build new townhouses everywhere not to fix up his own place, Dani thought. She tied Nikki to a parking meter after making sure there were no pizza crusts within reach. "Now there's nothing for you to be upset about, boy, 'cause we'll be right back." Nikki wagged his tail, knowing he could start his trademark howling as soon as the girls were out of sight.

Opening an old heavy wooden door, Dani and Caitlin stepped into a large, dark office. An elderly woman with a beehive hairdo sat with her back to the girls typing on an ancient typewriter. The office had high ceilings, and when Dani cleared her throat, the sound echoed loudly. Outside, Nikki's howls rang shrilly up and down Somerset. Dani waited a full thirty seconds before clearing her throat again. Without moving her head the woman with the beehive said, "I heard you the first time, and I've heard your hound every time." Then, spinning in her chair and drilling Dani with her bespectacled eyes, she said, "That's your dog, isn't it?"

"Yes, ma'am," Dani said, wishing it were otherwise.

The woman pushed her glasses down her nose. "Not sure I want to be a *ma'am*. The name's Lucy. What can I do you for?"

Dani could hear Nikki's howling over the traffic noise. "Um ... um ... please excuse me for a minute." She flew outside to the fury of Nikki's self-expression and meekly came back into the office to the same racket. "Poor little guy misses me."

"He's trained you well," Lucy said.

Caitlin grinned, and Dani puzzled over what the woman had meant until she remembered why they were there. "Well, Mrs. ... Miss ... Ms. ... Lucy, has Mr. Mitchell done anything suspicious lately, say, in the past week or so?"

Lucy chuckled and leaned her cone-shaped coiffure forward like the Leaning Tower of Pisa. "The man's whole life's suspicious. I should know. I've been his secretary, receptionist, and chief bottle washer for fifty years. You'd think I'd have learned by now. Come to think of it, he's been awfully irritated lately, even more than usual, if that's possible. Heard him mumbling the other day about wrecking some kid's sandcastle. I guess that's what brings you two here. I don't mind telling you, the old guy could use a little retribution, so tell me how I can help."

The lines on Dani's forehead that made her look like a Pekinese disappeared and the confident expression of a detective appeared. "Well, Lucy, you're absolutely right. You've guessed our reason for being here. You see, we found this matchbook at the scene of the crime, so to speak."

Lucy arched a carefully applied eyebrow. "That would be the sandbox?"

"Uh, yeah, sure," Dani said with a tad too much

enthusiasm. "The sandbox. What else could I mean? Anyway, we wondered if Mr. Mitchell dropped the matchbook somewhere."

"People generally call him Old Man Mitchell, more because of his temperament than his age. I'm six months younger, so I'm just Lucy. Now let me see. Mitchell fell on his rear end on a sandcastle and you found a book of matches. Seems like a no-brainer to me. Sure, that's his coat of arms on the matches. He has boxes of them. He smokes a pipe and goes through a book of matches an hour."

Dani's eyes narrowed. "Lucy, this is real important ..."

"Hey, I'm with you, honey. After all, don't they say that a woman's sandcastle is her castle, or something like that." Lucy chuckled. "Go on, dear."

Caitlin observed a pattern with previous cases and noted that they had to get to the bottom of who the *they* everybody kept referring to really were.

Dani put on her most serious detective stare and launched into interrogation mode. "Lucy, can you tell us where Mr. Mitchell was a little more than a week ago? Two Fridays ago, to be precise, in the evening?"

Lucy frowned. "I thought the sandcastle incident just happened a couple of days ago, but what the heck." She opened a large blue appointment book and scrutinized a series of entries, scratched-out entries, and re-entries. "Hmm, seems he was out with Jerry up at Kingsmere in Gatineau Park. And a little later the same night they had another meeting in Windsor Park."

"Wow!" the girls cried together.

"Does it say who they met?" Caitlin asked.

Lucy squinted at the appointment book. "'Fraid not."

When Dani was able to catch her breath, she asked,

"Lucy, we just have one more question."

Lucy heard the bay of the beagle yet again. "Shoot. Anything. Pronto."

"Who's Jerry?"

"Jerry Skinner is Old Man Mitchell's right-hand man. Jerry doesn't even light a match without Mitchell's say-so."

"Thanks, Lucy," Dani said, retreating toward the racket created by Nikki.

"If Jerry was left-handed, would he be Mr. Mitchell's left-hand man?" Caitlin asked for no apparent reason. "Or would that only happen if Mr. Mitchell was left-handed?"

Lucy snapped shut the big blue book. "They say you can go crazy asking too many questions, you know."

Caitlin started backing toward the exit. "*They* do, do *they*?" And then, realizing she had just asked another question, she nodded and was gone.

17
Detective Sadie Says

"Clever plan, don't you think?" Dani said over her shoulder, two strides ahead of her friend.

"Maybe, but you're going to have to be a whole lot more clever to beat Sadie at cribbage."

"Even seasoned detectives like us can't do the impossible," Dani said, kicking at a pile of leaves. Excitement in the air could be measured by the bounce in Dani's stride and the way she scattered heaps of leaves into the crisp Saturday morning air. She was thrilled about her plan to give Officer Farrell the evidence he needed to prove Old Man Mitchell was the murderer. Caitlin was delighted that they might finally be able to prevent a zillion townhouses from being built in her park. And if all that excitement wasn't exciting enough, the girls felt a tingle of anticipation, for tonight was Halloween!

"But, Dani," Caitlin said as loud as she could muster from behind her friend, "even if Officer Tom does come to Sadie's place, that still doesn't mean he'll believe we have enough evidence to get the two murdered people dug up or —" Caitlin wrinkled her nose. "What was that word?"

"Exhumed," Dani said in her best crime-show voice.

"Exhumed," Caitlin echoed. "Yuk. But, Dani, what if he doesn't believe us?"

"Then we use our secret weapon."

"And what would that be, Sherlock?"

"Why, that's elementary, my dear Watson. Sadie. Come on."

The girls walked along the corridors of Abbotsford Home, greeting the staff who were accustomed to seeing Sadie's favourite twelve-year-olds. For once Dani was determined to knock on the door to Sadie's room before she heard them approach, but just as Dani raised her fist, they heard a familiar squawk. "No use lurkin' around outside like a couple of beagle pups in the rain, girls. You know these old bones are in here."

"Darn, I was so close," Dani said under her breath as she opened the door.

"So close to what, Dani girl? You know if you say it I'll hear it," Sadie said.

"Guess I should know that by now."

I wonder if Sadie can hear me thinking, Caitlin thought. *I'd better be careful what I think.*

"Eh?" Sadie said. "What's on your mind, Caitlin? You have a look on your face like you're schemin'."

Dani glanced at her watch furtively, then checked it again.

"That's right, Dani," Sadie said, "it's five to ten, both times. Don't worry. Tom will be here at exactly 10:00 a.m. just like we planned. Now come over here and give this old bag of bones a proper Halloween hug." She extended a bony arm toward each of the girls.

They stepped forward and gave the crusty old woman a hug just as Officer Farrell filled the doorframe of her room. "Girls, you'll never win those loonies back consorting with the enemy like that," he said, removing his hat, stepping into the room, and planting a big kiss on Sadie's weathered forehead. "It took me years to realize that the *Great* in Great-Aunt refers to Sadie's greatness at winning loonies."

"Actually, we figured that out a long time ago," Caitlin said.

"We just like losing loonies," Dani added.

Sadie chuckled. "Now, children, just consider it an investment in your education."

"I wonder if we could study playing cribbage and detective work instead of going to school," Dani said.

"Oh, we're playing detective again, are we?" Tom said.

Dani's forehead wrinkled into her Pekinese expression as she struggled to find the right words to say. "It's not that we're *playing* detective, like pretending. I meant *playing* like learning a sport, 'cause we know that detective work is serious business."

"So count yourselves lucky, girls, that you're twelve and don't have to worry about being serious yet," Tom said.

Dani's forehead wrinkled even more. "But, but, but …"

Tom grinned, stretched, and yawned. "So how about our weekly cribbage lesson before I fall asleep? I worked the graveyard shift last night and I'm real tired. Come to think of it, the graveyard shift is the one to work this close to Halloween, isn't it?" Tom laughed until he noticed the expressions staring back at him. "Come on, girls, why the *grave* looks?" Pleased with himself, he pulled up a chair and sat down.

Dani blew out a couple gallons of air. "We didn't come here today to play cribbage."

"Oh, darn!" Caitlin said. "I feel lucky today and we could use a few loonies."

Dani's eyebrows knitted together as she whispered out of the side of her mouth, "Caitlin, get serious."

"You'll need more than luck to beat Sadie," Tom said.

Caitlin shrugged. "Don't we know it."

Dani glared at Caitlin, then looked at Tom. "The thing is, Officer Tom, well, I'll get to the heart of the matter …"

"Can you exhume people?" Caitlin blurted.

"Is that what this is about?" Tom asked. "Are you two still thinking there's been a murder on every street corner?"

"There aren't any street corners where these murders happened," Caitlin insisted.

"Officer Tom," Dani said fervently, "we now have the proof you need about the two murders. We wanted to tell you about it earlier this week, but school kind of got in the way."

"Girls, I know you're trying to help," Tom said with more than a trace of exasperation, "but I thought we were finished with that business. I thought we were going to have fun surrendering our loonies to Great-Aunt Sadie."

"But we do have proof," Caitlin said.

"And you did say you'd be able to investigate these murders if we got evidence," Dani said.

Tom's grin turned into a grimace. "Girls, what you might think is evidence hardly qualifies —"

"Now hear them out, Tom," Sadie snapped. "If these two say they've really got something, then it must be true. I'll vouch for 'em."

Tom whistled. "Oh, boy! Now you're bringing in the heavy guns. Okay, girls, what have you got?"

"Well, for one thing, a matchbook," Dani said.

Tom whistled again. "Wow!"

"You know I don't like sarcasm, Tom. Listen up!" Sadie scolded.

Officer Farrell glanced at his great-aunt sheepishly, then returned his attention to the girls. "Okay, explain."

"We've got a matchbook that was dropped by the murderer at Kingsmere just after the murders were committed," Dani said triumphantly. "And guess what coat of arms is on the matchbook."

"I bet you're going to tell me," Tom muttered, keeping one eye on Sadie, who was still glowering at him.

"The coat of arms is Old Man Mitchell's," Caitlin said. "And guess what company's building townhouses in Windsor Park and next to Gatineau Park?"

"Let me see. Could it be the Mitchell Development Company?" Tom said, wincing as he expected Sadie to upbraid him again. "So where's this matchbook?"

Dani bit her lip. "The thing is, we kind of forgot to bring it. But we can get it."

Tom ran a hand through his thick hair. "Girls, my captain took a piece off my hide the last time I went to him about this, so you'll have to come up with more than a book of matches for me to try anything again."

"No problem," Dani said. "If you talk to Lucy at the Mitchell Development Company office on Somerset Street, she'll tell you."

"And she'll show you in her big blue book," Caitlin added.

"Thank you, Caitlin," Dani said, a little irritated at her friend's intrusion. "Lucy will show you the appointment book, which says Old Man Mitchell, the owner of the Mitchell Development Company, was at the scene of the crime of at least one of the murders three Fridays ago and that he had another meeting the same night with someone in Windsor Park."

If Dani stood higher on her toes, she might bump her head, Caitlin thought.

Tom sat back in his chair and fidgeted with his hat. "If your Lucy can really do this, you may just have something, just maybe … but I still don't know. You should've heard my captain last time. No, on second thought, no one should ever hear him, particularly young girls, when he's that mad."

"Well," Sadie said decisively, "if you ever expect to make detective, Tom, you'll just have to follow the lead of these two fine sleuths."

Sadie winked at the girls as Tom groaned. "Great-Auntie, I'd like to say you're too old and these two are too young. I'd like to say, just leave it to the police and all the bad guys will get caught and no crime will go unpunished."

"But you're not my grandnephew for nothin', right?"

Tom sighed. "Right. If I've learned one thing from you, it's that sometimes you've got to roll the dice, take a risk, be completely foolish …"

"Good thinkin'," Sadie said, rubbing her hands together. "That reminds me. It's time for the four of us to get down to a rollickin' game of cribbage."

Tom got to his feet, towering over Sadie and the girls, and stretched. "I'd love to stay and contribute to the Sadie Squires loonie fund, but I've got work to do."

"That's the spirit," Sadie said. "The girls and I will take care of business here."

"Thanks, Officer Tom," Dani said.

Tom groaned again. "If I attempt to do what you're asking, it'll probably guarantee I'll walk a beat for the next thirty years."

Sadie snorted. "In thirty years you'll still be a pup."

"Good luck," Caitlin said as Tom tipped his hat and exited.

"Girls, you inspired Tom to take a risk and that's good. Now get your loonies, shake the dice, and let's do some more riskin', shall we?"

As Sadie set up the game, Caitlin whispered, "Where's the risk for Sadie to play us?"

"None whatsoever," Dani whispered back, "and she knows it."

For once Sadie pretended not to hear.

18
Old Man Murderer?

Nikki sprawled on Dani's bed, exhausted from sleeping all day.

"Guess Halloween doesn't get ol' Nikki too excited," Caitlin said, trying on her aunt's red wig.

"Sure, he's excited about Halloween," Dani protested.

Caitlin gazed at the ceiling. "Uh-huh."

"Look, I'll prove it. Watch carefully." Dani walked back and forth in front of Nikki. The loyal beagle never lifted his head but managed to follow his master dutifully with his eyes. "See, he's watching us and thinking exciting thoughts about Halloween."

"Oh, brother!" Caitlin said, applying gaudy makeup around her eyes.

Nikki also chose not to raise his head at the sound of four noisy teenagers thumping up the stairs.

"Looks like the children are still getting into costumes and playing childish games," Kathleen taunted in the doorway to Dani's room.

"I believe we gave up the practice of trick-or-treating in grade three," Samantha added.

Looming behind the elder sisters, Double J seemed shy and awkward in the presence of female company. As usual Pipsqueak Pete weaved and bobbed, first appearing under Kathleen's armpit and then over Samantha's shoulder.

"You're going to miss a lot of treats," Caitlin said.

Samantha sniffed. "Sugar products and greasy chips aren't worth standing in line and dressing like court jesters for."

"Getting dressed up is half the fun," Dani said.

"But only for the half-witted," Kathleen retorted.

Caitlin twirled in her 1960s go-go dancer costume. "Which reminds me, Dani. We're going trick-or-treating in half an hour and you haven't even said what you're wearing yet."

"That's 'cause it's a surprise, but I can show everyone now."

"I'm sure we don't care to know," Kathleen said.

"We're going to spend the evening reading books to each other," Pipsqueak announced. "Sounds like fun, don't you think?"

"Oh, joy," Caitlin said, suppressing a yawn.

"Whoopee," Dani said with an obvious lack of enthusiasm.

"Dani!" Dani's dad, John, shouted a floor below at the top of his well-developed lungs.

Nikki's head came to life and then the rest of his body flexed into a standing position. Just as John started a second scream, Nikki's howl drowned it out. The beagle's second howl snuffed out Dani's effort as she yelled back, "What is it, Dad?"

In a few seconds John was up the stairs. "What the devil! Bloody hound! Dani, get downstairs. That policeman's here again to see you and Caitlin!"

The girls scrambled down the stairs with Nikki tangled in their legs at every step. Tom Farrell stood in the hallway, grinning despite the dark bags under his eyes. "Well, girls, I've been on the case since I last saw you and now I'm really exhausted, but it's been worth it. Lucy confirmed that Mitchell and Jerry Skinner were both at Kingsmere three Fridays ago. And I've independently confirmed that later the same night Councillor Gertrude Owens also met with Mitchell and Skinner to discuss her opposition to their Windsor Park land deal. The long and the short of it is that Mitchell's been taken into custody for questioning. But more important, and after a whole lot of persuading from my captain, Judge Ross issued an order to exhume the bodies of both Owens and Williams. So once thorough autopsies have been conducted, we'll see whether we really do have foul play here."

The first noise issued from Double J since he had entered the house. The four teenagers were gathered at the top of the stairwell to listen, and when Double J heard what Officer Farrell said, he croaked, "Grandpa, a murderer?"

"And who are you?" Tom asked, looking up. "Why don't you come down here?"

"He's Old Man Mitchell's grandson," Pipsqueak answered, slithering down the stairs behind his gargantuan friend. "We both work for Mr. Mitchell doing whatever needs doing."

Tom slid his cap toward the back of his head and scratched one ear. "Quite a coincidence finding you here." He peered at Dani and Caitlin. "Right, girls?"

Dani gulped. "I guess we forgot to mention we kind of know Old Man Mitchell's grandson, Double J."

"And his friend, Pipsqueak Pete," Caitlin piped up.

"I see …" Tom glanced at Double J. "Your grandfather's only being questioned so far. We don't know if he's guilty of murder. In fact, we don't even know if we have any murders. But I think you and your friend should come down to the station with me, anyway, and answer a few questions."

Silence descended on the group.

Tom coughed, breaking the quiet. "And take it from me, son, even though he's your grandfather, please don't lie for him or else you could end up being charged as an accessory."

"It can't be true," Kathleen wailed. "Double J's grandfather has to be innocent."

"Pete, say something," Samantha urged Pipsqueak, who for the first time in his life was both motionless and speechless.

19
A Spooky Fashion Show

"That's it?" Caitlin asked with surprise. "That's your costume?"

"Yup," Dani answered proudly, modelling an oversized T-shirt she had pulled over her overalls. "Read it."

On the front of the T-shirt, Caitlin read: LAND DEVELOPERS IN PARKS ARE SPOOKY! The words were surrounded by a bunch of scary ghosts.

"Turn around," Caitlin said. "I can't wait to see the rest." On the back Dani's T-shirt read: DID YOU KNOW THAT THE CITY OF OTTAWA AND THE GOVERNMENT OF CANADA ARE SELLING *YOUR* PARKS TO LAND DEVELOPERS? WE'RE NOT KIDDING. THIS IS A GRAVE SITUATION! Around these words were gravestones and skulls, all neatly arranged.

"How come it says *we* if you're wearing the silly T-shirt?" Caitlin asked. When her friend didn't answer immediately, she said, "Oh, no, you didn't have one of those things made up for me? I've got my costume on."

"But, Caitlin, it's perfect," Dani pleaded, pulling another

T-shirt out of her drawer. "I knew you were going to be a go-go girl, and these shirts fit us just like miniskirts. Clever, don't you think?"

"A miniskirt over overalls is ridiculous."

"So I'll look ridiculous and you get to look like you're wearing a cool miniskirt."

"Dani, it doesn't look like a miniskirt. It looks like a baggy T-shirt, and I'm not wearing it!"

"Not even if it saves your park and my dad's old family farm from a zillion townhouses?" Dani asked, playing the guilt card.

"Wearing these dumb T-shirts won't save Windsor Park, Dani," Caitlin insisted, stamping her foot.

"But would you wear it if it could?"

"Of course, but —"

"Good," Dani said. "Better put it on then. And we don't have much time, 'cause the TV and newspaper people will be there soon."

"Where?"

"First, the mayor's house. The newspaper said politicians like kids trick-or-treating on Halloween. And the newspaper and TV people seemed real interested in our protest. They even said they were going to look into this story about parks."

Caitlin glanced at herself in the mirror. The baggy T-shirt sprawled over the costume she had spent so much time perfecting. "Dani, what in the world have you got us into this time?"

Caitlin had to admit that this time Dani seemed to have it all figured out. Her plan was actually a plan. She had found out that the mayor's home was located on the Rideau Canal, an easy walk from Caitlin's house. Caitlin still doubted that media people would be interested, but as they crested the hill and were in sight of the mayor's impressive house, the girls were swarmed. People from all the television networks and radio stations poked cameras and microphones at the girls. And there were plenty of reporters from the newspapers, too.

"Dani, you've been busy," Caitlin whispered. "I mean, really, really, really busy."

"Yes, I have," Dani said while smiling into one camera and then another. A reporter from the CBC told them she was glad Dani had called, because the transfer of parkland to the Mitchell Development Company was most unusual. A journalist from the *Globe and Mail* said the transfer of land adjacent to a federal park to the Mitchell Development Company was unprecedented. Then the reporters and camera jockeys positioned themselves around the front door to the mayor's house as Dani reached for the bell.

"How come there's no other kids here?" Caitlin asked.

A cameraman from a local TV station called the A-Channel said, "Kids never come here for Halloween. That's why the mayor keeps making the invitation."

A CTV news correspondent added, "It's well-known that the mayor really doesn't like kids."

"Oh, great!" Caitlin groaned. "Dani, let's get the heck —"

Then the front door opened dramatically, and a beaming Mayor Perkins appeared. He seemed pleased to see the cameras and reporters as he posed and his grin got even bigger. "Bill, Mike, Christine, come to see the mayor dole out the goods, have we?" he said, making eye contact with the reporters from CBC, CTV, and Global TV as if he had been expecting old friends. He held a large, full bowl of candy in front of Dani and Caitlin, but he didn't look at them. "Go on, kids, take one."

When the mayor realized the girls weren't taking any candy, he adjusted his glasses and peered at Dani and Caitlin. "You don't have any bags for candy, kids. And your costumes …" At that point Dani turned to display the message on her back. Perkins's scalp looked oily under the camera lights, and his face had red blotches. The mayor's breathing was laboured as he demanded, "What's the meaning of this? Who put you up to this? What do you hope to prove with these shenanigans?"

Dani thought, *We can't back down now*, as Caitlin wondered just how bad the T-shirt made her look on TV.

"Mr. Perkins, Mr. Mayor, Your Highness …" Dani began.

"Not Your Highness," Caitlin hissed. "He's not a queen. The mayor's called Your Worship, I think."

"Your Worship?" Dani said, puzzled. "I thought worshipping was only done in churches." But with the cameras rolling and the mayor fuming, Dani decided to leave the worship debate for another time. "Mr. Mayor, sir, even though we really do like trick-or-treating for candy —"

"It wouldn't hurt to take just one," Caitlin whispered, tentatively raising her hand toward the bowl.

Dani swatted Caitlin's hand away and glared at her friend. "This year we have more important business to attend to, right, Caitlin?" As the sweat on the mayor's face began to pool and cascade, Dani rose on her toes and was about to hook her thumbs under her overall straps when she noticed that her T-shirt made that impossible. "Darn, um, you see, sir, we don't think it's right to sell parks to pay for the deficit, 'cause once the parks are gone and the townhouses are built, we can never buy them back, even if the deficit's all paid off."

The mayor seemed confounded by this simple, direct kid's logic. He was a skilled man in the art of politics and decided the best defence was to obscure the issue and distort the facts. He had always lived by the motto, "There is no truth, only victory."

"Well, young ladies, at your tender age it's hard to understand politics, though I can see that you mean well." He thrust his smarmy smile into the thicket of cameras, and Dani thought of sharks. "If we didn't take care of the deficit, you wouldn't have schools. You wouldn't like that now, would you?"

Caitlin thought, *Does this guy realize he's talking to kids?*

"Or hospitals or shelters or food banks," the mayor continued. "You wouldn't want people to starve on the streets, would you?" The mayor sensed his opponents softening, could taste the tang of victory. "And I agree with you totally that it's a shame about Windsor Park. I personally wanted to keep it as it was, but the job of a mayor is nothing more than running meetings and fielding other people's opinions. Mayors have no real power, right, Mike?" Perkins winked at the guy from CTV and didn't seem to notice Dani struggling to extract a piece of paper from beneath her T-shirt and deep inside her overalls pocket. As Dani fidgeted, the mayor wiped at the oil slick on his bald head. "Sure is warm for Halloween, eh, Bill?" he said to the CBC man.

"Mr. Mayor?" Dani said from below the trajectory of the camera. "Mr. Mayor?"

"What can you do with kids today?" the mayor asked the assembled journalists. "You try to *treat* them and they try to *trick* you. And you can quote me, Christine," he added, flashing the Global TV woman a toothy smile.

"This isn't a trick," Caitlin said, hands on her hips. "I'd never wear something completely out of fashion as a trick."

"Mr. Mayor," Dani said, spreading out the paper she'd

finally excavated from her overalls, "according to these transcripts from City Council meetings, it was you who made the motion to sell city parkland three times." The mayor appeared more than a little annoyed and drew a breath to speak, but Dani held both the momentum and her chin. "And then the land was sold to the Mitchell Development Company without going to tender so that the city could get the money, even though Councillor Owens said the land was worth twice as much as it was sold for."

"What does *tender* mean?" Caitlin asked, scrunching up her nose.

"I think it means the city councillors don't have tender feelings for the land," Dani said out of the side of her mouth.

Caitlin nodded. "Makes sense."

A moth flew over Perkins's head, buzzing at the porch lamp that bathed his damp, oily scalp in unnatural light. The front door handle creaked from the grip of the mayor's left hand. After several lines of argument flashed through Perkins's boiling brain, he finally said, "The land was sold fair and square and now the city's deficit is gone. And if you think there's something wrong with doing that, why don't you go trick-or-treating at the prime minister's house, 'cause the federal government sold land next to one of their parks!" And with that fantastic suggestion, the mayor unceremoniously slammed the door closed with his left hand.

"Duh, as if," Caitlin said, hands back on her hips.

"Hey," Dani said, "how did he know?"

"Know what?"

"Where we're going to trick-or-treat next."

20
A Lesson in Politics

"The prime minister of Canada!" Dani said triumphantly.

And I always thought he was the prime minister of Timbuktu, Caitlin thought. Instead she said, "Dani, we can't trick-or-treat at *his* house!"

"Sure we can. Remember the newspaper said that both the mayor and the prime minister like kids trick-or-treating, and besides, the people from all the newspapers and TV stations really thought it was a good idea."

Caitlin groaned. "And I really thought it was a good idea to take a ride from the news people when they offered."

"It's better if we walk on our own," Dani said, already two strides ahead of her friend. "And if they should happen to be there when we arrive, it'll be another big coincidence." The girls scurried along the Rideau Canal toward the prime minister's residence on 24 Sussex Drive. Strong northern winds slowed their progress and sent mini-tornadoes of leaves into the air and across the canal water. Dani pumped her arms with determination and leaned far forward as gusts of wind blew in and out of her oversized T-shirt. Caitlin gathered her fashion monstrosity tightly to her side and skipped along, wondering if Dani's nose was touching the sidewalk yet. Over the wind and twirling leaves Caitlin shouted at Dani's hunched back. "How come the mayor and councillors didn't tender or have tender feelings about selling the parkland to Old Man Mitchell and nobody else?"

Dani lifted her nose from the pavement and turned her head. "It means something's rotten in the state of Denmark."

"Did the politicians sell the parks in Denmark, too?" Caitlin asked, alarmed.

"I think so. This guy named Hamlet was in a play once and he got real mad when his dad got murdered and his mother sold all the land and married a new king."

"Wow, what did Hamlet do?"

Dani had to think about the question for a minute. "He took action," Dani said, pounding her fist into her hand, "He went to the new king and told him what he thought and everyone got killed."

"I guess the prime minister's kind of like our king," Caitlin offered.

As Dani stopped in her tracks and her friend bumped into her back, the sound of Caitlin's groan was lost in the wind. "This guy Hamlet had to do something or else he couldn't live with himself, just like us," Dani said.

I could live with myself, Caitlin thought.

"But he fooled the king by having some actors act out the crime so the king would know he knew. You see, it was a play inside the play called *Hamlet*, kind of like we're doing a play for the mayor and the prime minister. See?"

"Oh, I see," Caitlin said, seeing nothing but the back of

Dani's billowing T-shirt. "So if Hamlet fooled the king, how come everyone still got killed?"

Dani pretended she couldn't hear her friend's question over the wind just in case it had anything to do with their trip to the prime minister's house.

"I guess we better be careful 'cause it could get dangerous," Dani said. "But most important, we don't want to be cowards, do we?"

To be or not to be, that's a heck of a good question, Caitlin thought, but decided to ask Dani another question. "Dani, if we can't be cowards, can we at least get candy this time?" However, Dani was now four strides ahead and the northern wind was swishing leaves around her ears so that the eternal question was forever lost.

Dani and Caitlin weren't the only kids who thought it would be a good idea to trick-or-treat at the prime minister's house. Standing for a moment at the entrance to the magnificent grounds, the girls spied a group of children waiting in awe at the house's bright open doorway. As first Dani and then Caitlin strolled down the long laneway, they heard the familiar voice of the prime minister himself.

With the news people from the mayor's house following them, Caitlin whispered hopefully, "Maybe he'll give us a couple of handfuls of candy before he reads our T-shirts."

Before Dani could answer, though, the prime minister's attention switched from his departing visitors to his new guests. "Well, well, Mike, Christine, Bill, you're too late for the scrum. We had that after Question Period today. I must admit I'd rather be on the news for giving candy to kids than for taking the heat in Parliament. How about some candy? Go ahead. The prime minister hands out candy to the press.

Pretty good, eh?" He offered his basket of candy.

After some of the media people politely chose a candy, the prime minister addressed Dani and Caitlin. "Now I know you two won't disappoint me by taking just one measly candy. Grab a handful — like this." The prime minister demonstrated for all the cameras.

When the girls didn't immediately plunge their hands into the basket, the leader of the land cocked his head and winked at Bill, the CBC man. "When I grew up the youngest of many children, if we were given the chance at such a fine basket of candies, we'd have jumped in with both feet. It's okay, girls, there are no parents here and I won't tell anyone."

"Sir, Your Honour, Your Excellency, Your Eminence!" Dani sputtered.

"What should we call you, sir?" Caitlin asked.

"Mr. Prime Minister will do. And what should I call you two?"

"I'm Your Highness," Caitlin said, "and my friend's called Empress."

The prime minister's eyebrows creased for a moment, then he decided Caitlin was joking. "Ha-ha, that's a good one! Cheeky. Maybe I should make you an ambassador."

Dani coughed politely. "Mr. Prime Minister, my name's Dani and this is my friend Caitlin and, well, the thing is, we didn't exactly come here for candy …"

Caitlin's hand, halfway to the candy basket, slowly and reluctantly returned to her side.

"Oh, I see," the prime minister said. "Perhaps you'd like my autograph. I could write on your T-shirts beside the gravestone there as long as it doesn't mark the end of my political career. I have to admit I'm a bit superstitious. Ha-ha."

"Well, Mr. Prime Minister, maybe you could write on our shirts that your government won't build townhouses next to Gatineau Park," Caitlin said brashly. Then she thought, *I'd really love one of the chocolate caramel bars in that basket.*

Confusion flashed across the prime minister's face. "Eh? What does your shirt say?"

Dani and Caitlin slowly rotated and revealed the message on the backs of their T-shirts. The jovial expression fled the prime minister's features instantly. His eyebrows bunched together, and for a moment he looked as if he was going to respond angrily, but then perhaps he remembered the forest of cameras in front of him and thought otherwise. He chuckled, then shrugged. "Even on my night off at home I get protesters. I'm afraid, kids, I don't know what you're talking about."

Dani huffed and puffed with frustration as she struggled to extract yet another piece of paper from a pocket in her overalls.

I hope I don't look as ridiculous as Dani, Caitlin thought before recoiling at her reflection in the prime minister's hallway mirror.

"Mr. Prime Minister," Dani began, clearing her throat, "your government allowed the National Capital Commission to sell a large piece of federal land next to Gatineau Park to a developer who intends to put townhouses on it. According to this committee report, that land should be made part of the park, in particular Kingsmere, which William Lyon Mackenzie King gave to the people of Canada."

"He was prime minister once, too," Caitlin said in a low voice.

The prime minister's exaggerated shrug made him look

like a turtle in search of a shell to hide his head. "You can't expect me to know every decision my government makes. It's a big job to run a country."

"Yes, sir, Mr. Prime Minister, it must be a very big job, but the thing is, my associate and I think this is a very important issue for all Canadians."

"And Canadian grandkids," Caitlin added.

The prime minister glanced up at the cameras, which were moving in closer. "It's true we have to think of future Canadian children. My parents had ten kids, so they had lots to think about, right?" He then turned to the cameras. "You two young ladies leave me your telephone numbers and I'll have one of my people look into this matter."

Dani rose on tiptoe. "Strictly speaking, Mr. Prime Minister, the land that was sold shouldn't have been sold by any government."

The prime minister sensed excitement growing in the media people and could already see the lead story on the news later that night. He wiped his forehead and smiled grandly into the cameras. "Tell you what, girls, I'll look into this personally and I'll meet you both again to let you know what's happening. Okay?"

"When?" Dani asked boldly.

"Are you sure you two aren't members of the opposition parties in disguise?" The prime minister's eyes travelled nervously back to the cameras. "Monday afternoon, just after Question Period in Parliament. I'll meet you at my office across the street from Parliament on Wellington Street in the Langevin Block on Monday. I'm sure your school will give you the day off for such an occasion. Don't worry, girls. On Monday we'll solve this problem, and as a bonus, I'll explain how politics works, too."

"Wow, for that we might need an adult," Dani said.

"Oh, sure, bring whoever you like," the prime minister said with a dismissive wave.

Both girls grinned from ear to ear, and the prime minister's crooked smile never looked prettier. "Satisfied?" he asked, savouring his public-relations coup as the girls nodded. "Now is there anything else I can help you with this evening, Your Highness and Madame Empress?" Without speaking or thinking, Caitlin raised one hand and scooped up a bunch of candies from the basket still held by the prime minister. "How about that? You two pulled a big trick on me and I still gave you a big treat. I'm quite a guy, eh?"

21
And in the News Tonight ...

"Something tells me you weren't thinking of bringing your dad when you told the prime minister we needed an adult to help us understand politics," Caitlin said.

Dani fidgeted with the remote beside Caitlin on the couch in Dani's living room. "No, we couldn't bring Dad. He'd pee his pants."

"Something tells me you weren't thinking of bringing Dustin Fairburn, even though he writes books about history and politics and stuff," Caitlin said, stuffing a chocolate caramel candy into her mouth.

"Nope. I kind of thought we should understand more and not less about politics when the prime minister explains it all to us."

"And something tells me you weren't thinking about our older, wiser sisters, even though they act more like adults than any adults in the entire world."

"Nope. They already know about everything, so it

wouldn't do much good."

"And something tells me you had someone in mind, someone who's an adult 'cause she's as old as the hills, but someone who can still think like a kid."

"Watson, you're a genius. Sadie's the only logical choice, don't you think?"

"Absolutely, Sherlock."

"Good, 'cause whatever we can't understand about politics from the prime minister, Sadie will explain to us."

"What's this?" Kathleen asked, descending the stairs, perfect posture, nose in the air.

She looks like she's on an escalator, Dani thought.

Kathleen practised her smile. "The kids go out trick-or-treating and come home and watch the news. Could it be they're growing up?"

Samantha snorted. "Not likely."

"Well, I think it's great for the girls to be watching the news," John said, appearing out of nowhere, "but I have to admit I'm a bit surprised myself."

"We thought we'd watch the news tonight, Dad, 'cause it's real educational," Dani said.

"And 'cause we're in it," Caitlin added.

"Yeah, right," Kathleen sniffed.

"Nice try," Samantha said dismissively.

The girls looked up with sheepish grins and were quickly forgotten by the swirl of activity. Kathleen and Samantha went into the kitchen to check on the progress of their homemade brownies. Double J, who was visiting, lumbered down the stairs to the kitchen, having just finished *A Tale of Two Cities* by Charles Dickens. Pipsqueak Pete slinked in the back door to the kitchen, having completed his errand to get fresh milk for the brownies. And John hurried to answer the unexpected ring of the front doorbell.

"Dani, Caitlin!" John cried. "Officer Farrell's here again!"

"Hi, Officer Tom," Dani said.

"Would you like to watch the news with us?" Caitlin offered.

"It's real educational," Dani said.

"No thanks, girls," Tom said, pushing his hat back on his head, "but I do have some good news about the case."

"Dani, turn down the sound on the TV," John said.

Dani muted the sound. "We're all ears."

The anchorman on the CBC news read in silence as Tom began. "Well, thanks to you two, I think we're making some headway on this case."

John's jaw dropped as the four teenagers listened from the kitchen.

"The autopsies confirmed that Councillor Owens and Guy Williams died due to a slow-acting poison and not because of heart attacks." Deep gasps for air ensued, but Tom held up his hand. "That's not all. After investigating the lead you gave us about the Mitchell Development Company, Mr. Mitchell was officially arrested and charged with two counts of murder about an hour ago."

Tom seemed surprised when Double J thundered from the kitchen. "Grandpa didn't do it!"

For John the second shock registered a perfect 10 on the Richter scale. "Girls, that … that isn't … that can't be, and what the devil are you two doing on the news?"

Kathleen pointed a shaky finger at the television. "And … and … with the prime minister!"

By this point, John couldn't speak, but thanks to his waving arms, Dani figured that he wanted the sound turned up. The volume came on just in time for them to hear

Dani read to the prime minister from the paper extracted from her overalls. The screen showed the look of disgust on Caitlin's face as she saw the reflection of herself in her oversized T-shirt in the prime minister's hall mirror. The camera then moved in for a close-up of the prime minister's anguished face before his features softened and he promised to meet the girls in his office on Monday. The prime minister put one arm around each girl and all three smiled into the camera. As the news anchor chuckled at the prime minister's grave political problem, a stunned Samantha said, "Those T-shirts are ridiculous."

Caitlin spat out the French braid she was chewing on. "I know. I can't show my face at school after wearing that thing."

"But it worked," Dani said, switching channels to CTV.

The CTV anchor said the two young trick-or-treaters had effectively dropped a political bombshell on the prime minister's doorstep. The on-the-spot reporter added that the girls had done a better job than any protest groups had accomplished since the prime minister had come into office. "Never in thirty years has this reporter seen such evidence of the federal government selling a large piece of federal land adjacent to a federal park to a land developer. Who knows? If this trend continues, perhaps in five years Parliament Hill might also be crowded with cozy little townhouses, not to mention great national parks such as Banff and Jasper."

Dani zapped the television off, and before the volcano of questions erupted, Pipsqueak slipped between Double J and Kathleen with a tray of brownies. "No use letting a little mayhem and murder stop us from eating these while they're hot."

"Thanks!" Caitlin said enthusiastically.

"But how in the world did you two manage …" Samantha began.

"It just doesn't make sense," Kathleen interjected.

John got to his feet, then sat down, then stood again. "Dani, how, what, why … did you know …? You girls are going to be the death of me!"

"How are the brownies?" Pipsqueak asked.

"I tell you Grandpa couldn't have done it!" Double J cried. "He couldn't have murdered those two people because he was with me!"

"The brownies are yummy," Caitlin said, having already devoured two.

Tom sighed. "I appreciate you wanting to help your grandpa, son, but you never said anything about being with him when you came down to the station earlier today."

"It's true!" Double J said, becoming more animated than he had ever been in his entire life. "I was with Grandpa when we had those meetings with Councillor Owens and that NCC man."

Everyone was quiet, anxious to hear what the gentle giant would say next. Double J took a deep breath and spoke in a clear voice. "I should have said something before, but I was afraid for Grandpa and myself. But if it's true that someone from the Mitchell Development Company murdered those people, then I know who it was."

All eyes were riveted on Double J, and no one noticed Caitlin sneak another brownie from Pipsqueak's willing plate.

22
The Cradle of Power

"Dani, I hope you're not thinking of wearing dirty overalls!" John called out from the floor below.

"No, Dad," Dani dutifully answered. Then, to Caitlin, she said, "I just washed my overalls and they're looking pretty good, don't you think?"

Caitlin stood in front of the mirror in Dani's bedroom, trying to decide among three perfect matching outfits for their Monday meeting with the prime minister. "Dani, do you think I should wear this blouse and skirt together, or should I switch this white blouse for that blue one? Or should I wear this beige skirt? Maybe they're both wrong." Caitlin's face scrunched up with indecision.

Dani surveyed the situation and yawned. "I think what you're wearing is fine."

"Dani!" John shouted. "Officer Farrell's here to pick you up."

"Maybe I should ask Officer Tom and your dad what

they think," Caitlin said.

Dani levelled her worst evil eye at her best friend.

"Or maybe Nikki," Caitlin said, glancing at the beagle sleeping on Dani's bed. "Hmm, maybe not. Okay, this'll do."

John recited a steady stream of instructions and suggestions soon to be forgotten as the girls came downstairs and hurried into Tom's waiting police cruiser.

"Have you got all that, Dani?" John asked, breathless and frantic on the sidewalk.

"Right, Dad. Every word."

"Okay, so what did I say?"

"I could tell you, Dad, but gosh, look at the time."

John's faced twitched as he raised his watch. "Well, for goodness sake, get going, and remember what I said. Bye, girls." He slammed the cruiser door as if he had just secured the capture of two hardened criminals.

"Hello, girls," Tom said.

"Howdy, girls," Sadie chimed in, chuckling. "Now, Dani, you shouldn't toy with your father like that, poor thing."

"I know," Dani said, grinning, "but he makes it so easy."

"Are you nervous, Sadie?" Caitlin asked, smoothing out her skirt and wishing she had opted for the lavender one.

"About meetin' the prime minister?" Sadie said. "Why, he's just a fella with a bunch of warts and bumps like the rest of us. There's nothin' or nobody to be nervous about on this green earth as long as you're honest with yourself. And you two are about as honest as they come."

"What about me, Great-Aunt?" Tom asked.

"Better than most, I suppose," Sadie said with a mysterious smile. "But best not to ask for a comparison in the present company."

Tom sighed. "Well, I can honestly say I'm confused

about this case. Mitchell's grandson has made a statement that he waited in the car with his grandfather when they went to the meetings with Councillor Owens and Guy Williams. Mitchell concurs with his grandson's statement, but as the person accused of murder, you'd expect that. Double J and his grandfather maintain that Jerry Skinner visited the victims alone, then returned to the car and reported that his 'mission' had been accomplished. Skinner swears he's never even met Owens and Williams. I just hope for the sake of Mitchell's grandson that he's not lying to save his grandfather. I understand that the old gent is the only family the kid has."

Dani seemed distracted as she fidgeted with her seat belt and overall straps.

"Tarnation, girl!" Sadie said. "You're squirmin' like a beagle with a bad case of fleas."

"Could be the snake I put down her overalls," Caitlin said.

"I know it's down here somewhere," Dani mumbled, taking her lucky oval stone from her lower right pocket and placing it in her upper left pocket.

"I guess those overalls are like a filing cabinet," Caitlin said. "You just need letters on each pocket to know where to put stuff."

Dani stopped fussing for a moment and looked up. "You know, that's not a bad idea."

Caitlin rolled her eyes as Dani plunged her hands through her straps and back into her pockets. With a grunt and an elbow into Caitlin's side, Dani pulled a clear plastic bag out of her pocket. "Here it is," she said triumphantly. When no one asked what "it" was, Dani turned up the volume. "Here it is!"

"Okay, I'll bite," Tom said, peering into the rearview mirror. "What is it?"

"Could be nothing," Dani began.

Caitlin groaned. "Your elbow sure felt like something."

"Or it could be evidence," Dani added.

Tom raised an eyebrow. "Oh?"

"We found it at Mackenzie King Estate close to where that Williams guy was poisoned," Dani said.

"What is it?" Tom slammed on the brakes and stopped mere centimetres behind the car in front. "Sorry, everybody, I shouldn't have been looking in the rearview mirror. But, darn it, Dani, tell me what you've got there."

"A matchbook," Dani said. "We told you about it before, but we forgot to bring it to Sadie's place, remember? It has the Mitchell family coat of arms on it." She handed the plastic bag to Tom as the Peace Tower and Parliament Buildings came into view.

Tom held up the bag and peered inside. "I imagine it's pretty contaminated, what with your fingerprints on it and who knows who else's. Plus its discovery is more than a little irregular. But I'll take it back to our lab and have it checked for fingerprints, anyway. Now let's get you three to your big meeting."

A quartet of the prime minister's aides was waiting for the special guests when they filed into the Langevin Block on Wellington Street. Quick glances were exchanged at the presence of Sadie, the centenarian, but not a word was spoken. The three friends were then whisked away into the bowels of the building as the aides apologized to Sadie for the need for haste.

"No matter," Sadie said. "It's about time I had my daily

constitutional." She chuckled, then whispered to Dani and Caitlin, "Pomp and ceremony, girls. Just keep a level head and you can't go wrong."

As the group reached a sign proclaiming OFFICE OF THE PRIME MINISTER OF CANADA, the hallway came alive with the sound of scurrying people. Cameras and media people followed close on the heels of the prime minister in full flight on his way back from the House of Commons. Despite his hurried stride, he appeared to enjoy the pursuit. However, as soon as the reporters caught sight of Sadie and the girls standing behind the aides, the prime minister was left performing to an audience of no one.

"What do you plan to ask the prime minister today?" the CBC reporter barked.

"What do you think the prime minister plans to tell you today?" the CTV correspondent shouted.

"What do you think your grandmother plans to tell the prime minister today?" the Global TV journalist yelled.

The girls looked at each other, then glanced at Sadie in puzzlement. More questions flew and cameras clicked and rolled until Sadie dramatically raised a bony arm like a magic wand and snapped her fingers. During the silence that followed, Sadie adjusted her false teeth. "Ladies and gentlemen, these two fine girls have got a message and a mission for our prime minister and they asked me along because we're special friends. So listen to what they have to say. I guarantee it'll be the truth and that it comes from the heart."

Before anyone could say anything else, one of the prime minister's aides informed the media people that they wouldn't be allowed into the Prime Minister's Office. Then the prime minister stepped forward and shrugged. "I'm sorry, ladies and gentlemen. We're doing this because we don't want our guests to be shy with me."

Sadie's eyes narrowed. "Oh, I promise you, Mr. Prime Minister, shy we won't be, cameras or no cameras."

The girls each placed a hand on Sadie's thin forearm to calm their friend.

Inside the office the trio was invited to sit in deep leather chairs in front of a large oak desk. A fellow by the name of Hastings sat close to the prime minister on the other side of the desk. Hastings whispered into the prime minister's ear as Sadie scowled. She cupped a hand to her mouth first to Caitlin on her left and then to Dani on her right. "Can't trust a body that tells secrets right in front of your nose."

Dani grinned. "Shhh, Sadie!"

The prime minister nodded at the nervous-looking Hastings before turning his attention to Sadie and the girls. "I see you've brought your grandmother. That's nice."

"I'm not the girls' grandmother. I'm their friend."

The prime minister ignored Sadie's remark. "Well, I'm sure you'll agree, madam, that my government has acted very quickly to fix this little problem that's been brought to my attention. One of my ministers will make sure no townhouses are built anywhere near Gatineau Park. So that's good news, eh? Now do you have anything to tell me?"

"The chocolate caramel bars you gave out last night were real good," Caitlin volunteered.

The prime minister slapped his desk and laughed as Hastings twitched. "That's wonderful. Ha-ha! I give out all kinds of great treats, don't I? Well, I guess that's all we need to talk about then."

Hastings rose and announced that the prime minister had another meeting.

"Well, there is something else …" Dani began, struggling to formulate her thoughts.

Hastings beckoned Sadie and the girls to follow him out of the office.

"The child's not finished yet," Sadie said icily to Hastings.

The prime minister motioned at the ever-fluttering Hastings to sit down.

"The thing is, Mr. Prime Minister …"

The prime minister raised an expectant eyebrow. "Yes …?"

"Well, I'm real glad there won't be townhouses next to Gatineau Park, but I still wonder why your government sold the land in the first place when it wasn't supposed to sell it."

Hastings frantically whispered in the prime minister's ear as the leader of the land clapped his hands. "You really are cheeky, aren't you?"

"The child asked a good question," Sadie said. "I wondered the same thing myself."

"Well, my young friends and Madam Grandmother," the prime minister said with mounting exasperation, "you can't truly understand how politics works and nobody can blame you for that."

"Perhaps you can explain for the edification of the children and this old bag of bones," Sadie said archly.

"Of course, madam. It will be my pleasure."

"The land next to Gatineau Park, sir," Dani prompted.

"Yes, the land, of course. Let me tell you, there's no prouder Canadian in Canada than the man who sits before you. To be honest, the sale of that land was a mistake."

Sadie adjusted the glasses dangling from the end of her nose. "The child asked why your government sold land that belonged to the citizens of Canada without the consent of Canadians."

"Madam, we *are* the government elected by a plurality of Canadians."

"But people who voted for you didn't even know about selling the land," Dani objected.

The prime minister held up his hand to the ever-whispering Hastings. "A government doesn't consult with people on every matter before it."

Caitlin forgot all about the prime minister's delectable chocolate caramel bars. "But parks are the most important thing in Canada — after people and animals!"

The prime shrugged and grinned crookedly. "Most Canadians are more interested in their pocketbooks. But at your age, of course, you're still naive."

"Shame on you!" Sadie said, struggling to stand as she wagged a bony finger. "You should know better at your age than to fill these honest young girls with excuses and cynicism. Come on, Dani, Caitlin, let's see if our media friends outside are still waitin'."

The prime minister blanched, while Hastings tried to block the girls' and Sadie's exit.

"I give you my word that there will be no more shenanigans with federal parkland," the prime minister nearly gasped. "What could be better than that, eh?" When no one answered immediately, the leader of the land sagged, then sighed. "So what do you want?"

Sadie rubbed her bony hands together. "Now we're gettin' somewhere. Girls?" She looked at Dani, then at Caitlin, and each nodded as Sadie continued. "We figure the best way for this political boondoggle not to happen again is for you to step outside this room and tell those media folk that you and your government were dishonest and tried to pull a fast one on the Canadian people."

Hastings grimaced as he raised his hands to his ears.

"That way," Dani added, "you can tell the media that you're real sorry."

"And that you'll never do it again," Caitlin contributed.

"And that your government will do everything honestly from now on," Dani said triumphantly.

"And we'll tell the media that we think you're honest, after all," Caitlin said cheerfully. "And we'll also tell everybody that your chocolate caramel bars are the best in the country."

The prime minister waved off the trembling Hastings. "Anything else?"

"Well," Dani said hesitantly, stroking her chin, "there's one thing that would be real cool, not that we expect —"

"Come on, spit it out," the prime minister said impatiently. "By now I know you're not shy."

"How about putting up a statue of Prime Minister Mackenzie King next to the one of his old pal Bert Harper on Parliament Hill?"

"I think we already have a statue of Mackenzie King on the Hill, but still, that's not a bad idea. What do you think, Hastings?"

Hastings nodded nervously, for once in agreement.

The prime minister stared at the three visitors warily. "So is that it?"

Sadie and the girls nodded.

"Okay, then let's announce all this to the press outside." The prime minister got up and started toward the office door.

"You're doing the right thing," Sadie said.

As the door opened to a torrent of questions, the prime minister turned to Sadie. "Madam, when you want to come out of retirement and work for me as a cabinet minister, let me know, okay?"

Sadie chuckled. "Depends on whether you allow cribbage breaks."

The next day the front pages of every newspaper in Canada showed a perplexed prime minister pondering the idea of cribbage as a recreation activity for cabinet ministers.

23
Party at City Hall

Tom Farrell's grin was almost as wide as the front doorway to Dani's house as he entered her home the day after the girls' big meeting with the prime minister. "Do I have news!" he announced, pulling his hat off his head. "By the way, girls, nice to see you on the news again. Anyway, turns out we did get an interesting set of fingerprints off that matchbook you found, and darn if they don't belong to Jerry Skinner."

"Matchbook?" Dani's dad, John, asked from a group that included Kathleen and Samantha, as well as Double J and Pipsqueak, who had arrived just before Tom.

"So," Tom continued, ignoring the confusion on John's face, "Mr. Skinner's been officially charged with two counts of murder in the first degree. With the testimony of Dani, Caitlin, Double J, and Lucy at Old Man Mitchell's company, we have a pretty good case, I think, though I'm still hoping to get a confession out of Skinner. The matchbook really won't be admissible in court given how we came into possession of it. The real unanswered question, however, and one that might weaken our case, is the lack of a motive on Skinner's part. After all, Double J's grandfather owned a hundred percent of the company and Jerry was only a salaried employee. We'll keep digging, though, and like I said, Skinner might just break down and confess."

At that moment Double J coughed, and everyone stared at the shy teenager, who finally spoke. "Jerry Skinner had plenty of motive to commit murder. There was an agreement between him and my grandfather that if he got this development deal past the various governments, Grandpa would give him fifty percent of the company. When I told Grandpa I wanted to go to university to study English literature and someday become a professor, he had his lawyer draw up an agreement with Jerry. Grandpa was worried that he was getting too old and there was no one to take over his company."

Tom whistled. "That certainly sounds like a motive to me."

Pipsqueak popped up beside his immense friend. "But there's more news, right, Double J?"

Double J nodded slowly. "Grandpa just got out of jail and called to ask if you'd all come down to City Hall for an announcement tonight."

"Something's up," Pipsqueak said, "and it's got to be big if it's at City Hall."

"What time?" John asked.

"Six-thirty," Pipsqueak said.

"What do you think, Dad?" Dani asked.

"It's already six o'clock, Dani," John said. "I don't think there's enough time or room in our van."

"I can help with both," Tom volunteered. "There's lots of room in my cruiser."

"But how can you help with the time?" John asked.

"Ah," Tom said, grinning. "To address the issue of time, you've got to follow me and suspend all your instincts about what to do at a red light." John gulped as Tom slapped him on the back. "Trust me."

Dani pounded her fist into her other hand. "Come on, everybody, we're going to a party at City Hall!"

Mayor Perkins seemed uncomfortable standing, sweating, and grimacing in front of the microphone. Next to him, Old Man Mitchell, however, looked supremely content.

"Is Old Man Mitchell actually smiling?" Caitlin asked Dani.

The mayor's introductory coughing nearly choked him, then he launched into his speech. "Ladies and gentlemen, I realize this press conference was called on short notice. However, I believe it's important to clarify the city's position on an important matter in view of the prime minister's statement yesterday." The mayor dabbed a handkerchief on his oily scalp and sighed deeply. "Due to the recent controversy surrounding the sale and development of Windsor Park, I am hereby announcing that the City of Ottawa has reversed its decision and will not sell this or any other park now or in the future."

"Aw, heck, Perkins!" Old Man Mitchell snapped as he stepped to the microphone. "Controversy? I'd say disaster's a better word for this mess, and I know I have to bear most of the blame. I couldn't see the park for the townhouses." Mitchell chuckled at his little joke. "A city and a country need to keep their parks. We can always find more space for townhouses, close to parks, but not in 'em. You see, I had a little change of heart sittin' in a jail cell recently. Even though

I wasn't guilty of murder, the time in my cell was good for me. I had a chance to think about life, about what I've accomplished, and I've got to admit, I didn't much like what I saw. I've worked hard and I've had a profitable company for over fifty years, but I forgot something. I forgot to play. That's right. I'm eighty-one years old and I'm tellin' you that's what I'm gonna do from now on — *play!*" Mitchell peered into the crowd. "Popeye, get up here."

Caitlin's and Dani's eyes widened as the old guy Mitchell had fought with in Windsor Park elbowed and squinted his way through the confused crowd.

"This here's Popeye, and we met a while ago under peculiar circumstances. Fact is, he and I have become friends. And we think parks in this town could use a jolt of cash to help with the playin' that happens in 'em. So today I'm donatin' a million dollars to the city for its parks as long as decisions about spendin' are made through Popeye and me. Of course, two people decidin' don't always agree, so to keep us from fightin', I'm askin' my grandson, Double J, to come up here so we can ask him to chair our Fun Committee." As everyone practically shoved Double J up to the podium, Mitchell added, "Ah, heck, might as well bring that scrawny friend of yours, too, Double J."

Pipsqueak and Double J joined Mitchell and Popeye on the stage as Caitlin jabbed Dani in the ribs. "Know what's still missing, Sherlock?"

"What do you mean, Watson?"

"Don't you think we need to pay someone a visit before this night's done?"

"Ah, I see what you mean, Watson. It's time for another trip to Kingsmere."

"Only how do we get up there this late?"

Dani pulled on her overall straps. "Well, let's put it this way, Watson, my dad's about to think that it's his idea to suddenly drive up to Kingsmere."

"It's so easy, Dani, that it seems kind of cruel, don't you think?"

"Caitlin, you've been listening to Sadie too much. Besides, you heard Old Man Mitchell. It's time to *play*!

24

The Three Musketeers Ride Again!

Nikki and the girls walked down the path to Kingswood Cottage on the lake, while John headed up the hill toward the old O'Neill Farm.

"Your dad seemed a little confused by his sudden decision to drive up here, but he didn't waste any time," Caitlin said as she skipped along behind Dani.

"Yeah, he had this brilliant idea about visiting ghosts up at the O'Neill Farm now that the townhouses aren't going to be built."

"Really," Caitlin said, catching up to her friend, "and where do you suppose he got the idea about ghosts?"

Dani grinned until a howling Nikki met a barking Pat, who walked through Nikki's snout and out the other end.

"Maybe Nikki howls so much 'cause he has digestive problems," Caitlin speculated. "And if it's true that you are what you eat, it's no wonder Nikki's hungry all the time 'cause nothing stays in him."

Dani shook her head as she spied the former prime minister heading their way.

"And do you think Nikki could be a Chinese dog, Dani?" Caitlin burbled on.

"I'm afraid to ask," Dani said, "but here goes. Why do you think Nikki might be a Chinese dog?"

"'Cause I'll bet an hour after eating Pat, Nikki will be hungry again!"

Dani groaned and rolled her eyes while King appeared to be stricken with confusion.

"Don't worry, Mr. King," Caitlin said. "That was a joke."

"I thought as much," King said, finally smiling.

Dani stood on tiptoe and gripped the straps of her overalls. "Well, Mr. King, we did it!"

King now looked truly confounded. "Oh?"

Caitlin scrunched up her face. "Do you mean you don't know what's been going on the past few days?"

King blinked and remained expressionless. "Do you have something to tell me, girls?"

"We solved the murders!" both girls shouted.

"And stopped the townhouses!" Caitlin added herself.

"And the O'Neill Farm's going to become part of Kingsmere," Dani said.

"And Windsor Park's not going to be sold," Caitlin concluded.

Pat cocked his head to the right as King inclined his head to the left in a true picture of absolute puzzlement.

"We thought somehow you already knew," Caitlin said, a little miffed.

"But now that you do know, you don't seem too impressed," Dani said, deflated and flat-footed.

A crinkle around the former prime minister's eyes betrayed the beginning of a smile.

"You've been fooling us!" Caitlin cried. "You really have learned how to kid people."

King didn't just smile. He grinned. "Got you! It's called wearing a poker face." When the girls didn't respond, he added, "Which I must admit is the only face I wore throughout my entire life and death."

"Well, at least no one could tell what you were thinking at your funeral," Caitlin said nonsensically.

"Since meeting you two fine young ladies, I find it increasingly difficult to keep a poker face. I feel myself wanting to smile all the time, and since learning that you succeeded in your mission, I … I have to admit I'm positively giddy with joy." King got slightly serious for a moment. "However much I'd love to exchange pleasantries, though, you must both hurry."

The girls cocked their heads and said in unison, "Huh?"

"Your current prime minister is holding a press conference and making a formal announcement in an hour."

'This late at night?" Dani asked.

"You're pulling our legs again, aren't you, Mr. King?" Caitlin said.

"*Omigosh!*" Dani cried. "The prime minister's announcing a statue for you, isn't he?"

King bit his lip and nodded.

Dani began striding away, talking over her shoulder. "Come on, Caitlin. We have to collect Dad right away. He's about to re-alize he really needs to get back to the city in a hurry."

"And he doesn't even know it yet, poor guy," Caitlin said, skipping behind her friend.

The girls covered the short distance to the old O'Neill

Farm in world-record time. John stood with his back to the girls, staring at a fixed spot in the moonlit distance. Dani had to say "Dad" three times, then place a hand on his forearm before he noticed them.

When he turned, his eyes were moist. "I sure am relieved there won't be townhouses on the old family farm."

"Dad?"

John returned his attention to a clump of maple trees across the meadow that were illuminated by the full moon. "You know, girls, there's something about this place that, well, speaks to me."

"Dad, we have to go."

"I know it sounds silly, but it's almost as if I can sense the presence of our ancestors' spirits here. Did you girls know that last Sunday, November 1, was All Saints' Day, and that yesterday was All Souls' Day? For more than a thousand years, people have venerated their saints on November 1 and have honoured their dead ancestors and relatives. And on November 2 they've prayed for generations for those souls who have sinned but who might yet attain peace in heaven. That's how the whole tradition of Halloween began. Halloween means All Hallows' Eve, *hallow* is an ancient word that means 'holy person' or 'saint,' and Halloween is the night before All Saints' Day."

"That's real interesting, Dad, but we've got to go. Besides, aren't you too old to believe in ghosts?"

John took a deep breath. "Yes, I guess you're right. I suppose it's kind of silly of me to be out here half expecting to see a ghost."

"You have no idea, Dad."

"Maybe it's 'cause you have a restless spirit, sir."

"Yeah, that's it," John said, nodding. "So where are we

off to now?"

Just as the three began to turn away from the meadow, leaves started swirling upward in front of the maple trees. More and more leaves were swept into the vortex of a spontaneous mini-tornado, though strangely all around the dancing leaves there was absolute calm. As the spiral of leaves climbed above the tallest maple, it gracefully collapsed, wafting downward until all was still again.

John was the first to recover and speak. "Maybe it's not too late. Maybe I'm not too old to believe."

"That's the *spirit*!" Caitlin said.

Dani stamped her foot. "Dad, if we don't leave right away …"

"Parliament Hill will look like a ghost town," Caitlin finished.

By the time John and the girls arrived, Parliament Hill was indeed a ghost town. The current prime minister had already announced that a statue of William Lyon Mackenzie King, his illustrious if somewhat neglected predecessor, was to be commissioned and that it would be erected next to the one of King's best friend, Bert Harper. The two musketeers would again be united after all these years!

The press conference had taken place at the very spot where the King statue would be placed. Now only three lone figures remained from the crowd that had assembled earlier. John and the girls joined the William Lyon Mackenzie King Fan Club in front of a platform constructed to mark the location where the statue would soon be raised. The fan club's members seemed at first not to notice the three newcomers as they hotly debated the finer points of how the statue should look.

The Boy Scout was adamant that King should stand with both hands proudly holding the lapels of his suit coat. The ferret man wanted King's right arm extended dramatically, while the white-haired woman thought the old prime minister should be seated as if he were still in the House of Commons.

"But unless he's standing, what's the point of having him looking over Bert Harper's statue?" the Boy Scout demanded, stamping his foot with exasperation.

"And unless he has one arm in the air, how will Bert know he's even there?" the ferret man asked.

"That's idiotic!" the Boy Scout said. "Of course, he won't know King's there. We're talking about statues."

"Now, as president of this fan club, I may have to insist on a vote," the white-haired woman said.

"Dad, this is the Mackenzie King Fan Club," Dani whispered.

"Too weird for words," John said.

"Did the prime minister ask your fan club to decide how the statue should look?" Caitlin asked.

All three club members stopped arguing and peered at the intruding trio. "No," the Boy Scout said, "but we're confident our club will be consulted. After all, it's because of our letter-writing campaign that the prime minister commissioned this statue in the first place."

"Funny that the prime minister never mentioned anything about us during the press conference," the ferret man said, scratching his beard and his ferret.

"Could be because of the pressure we exerted," the white-haired woman speculated.

"Maybe we'll get an official letter from the prime minister asking us to participate in a committee," the ferret man said.

"Well, if we do, we'd better resolve among ourselves how Prime Minister King will pose," the Boy Scout said. "I say it should be like this — dignified." He thrust his chin in the air and clenched his hands on imaginary lapels.

As the ferret man, the white-haired woman, and John observed the Boy Scout's determined stance, the girls noticed something moving on the platform in the background. King himself, or at least his ghost, stood there holding and petting Pat as he grinned with amusement at the theatrics at his feet. The girls giggled as Pat wagged his tail and Rex's grin got bigger and bigger.

John and the members of the Mackenzie King Fan Club turned to the giggling girls. The Boy Scout unclenched his fists from his imaginary lapels and said, "I suppose you two have a better idea how our esteemed former prime minister should pose for future generations?"

"Well, I'm not too sure about future generations," Dani said, grabbing her overall straps as if they were lapels, "but I think he should stand kind of relaxed, wearing his old hiking shorts, and he should be holding his dog, Pat, 'cause Rex really loved that dog."

"And the sign on the statue should say: GOOD OL' REX AND HIS DOG, PAT, A PRIME MINISTER'S BEST FRIEND," Caitlin said.

"And then Bert, Rex, and Pat can be the three musketeers," Dani added.

"That's preposterous!" the Boy Scout exploded.

"I like it," the ferret man said.

"We'll have to consider this carefully," the white-haired woman said.

The Boy Scout glared at his fellow fan club members. "You can't be serious!"

At that precise moment Rex began a deep belly laugh, and naturally so, too, did the girls.

The Boy Scout kicked at a clump of grass. "And his best friend was Bert Harper, not his bloody dog!"

The ferret man started to giggle, then John joined in the laughter. Even the white-haired woman let loose with a few sniggers.

"I think ol' Bert will understand," Caitlin squeezed out between swells of laughter. "And the statue shouldn't make Rex too serious."

"His name wasn't Rex and he was very, very serious!" the Boy Scout insisted.

"Well, his friends called him Rex and we're all his friends, right?" Dani reasoned.

"And, besides, he's tired of being serious," Caitlin said, "so I think his statue should show him laughing, like he's just told the best joke in the world!"

Everyone, including Rex, laughed uproariously. However, the Boy Scout continued to protest.

"Too late," the white-haired woman said. "All in favour of a laughing statue of King holding his dog, Pat, say aye."

The white-haired woman and the ferret man cried, "Aye" as the Boy Scout shouted "No!"

"Motion carried!" the white-haired woman finally declared.

Over the guffawing and arguing that followed, Rex mouthed the words "Thank you" as he waved one of Pat's paws.

As the debate among the fan club members raged, the girls heard the Boy Scout protest, "But King *never* laughed!"

The girls turned to each other and smiled knowingly. The feuding fan club almost distracted Dani and Caitlin from the fact that the platform was now empty. As tempers continued to flare, the girls each took a deep breath and sighed.

"Guess Rex is gone off to visit his old pal Bert Harper," Dani said.

"Guess he fooled us by disappearing when we weren't looking so that we wouldn't get all teary-eyed when we said goodbye," Caitlin said, her eyes getting moist.

The Boy Scout stamped his feet once more and shouted, "Next you'll be telling me Mackenzie King was the funniest man in Canada!"

"You've got that right!" Dani and Caitlin roared as they burst into another fit of uncontrollable laughter.